KITTY CAT

AGE OF NIGHT BOOK ONE

MAY SAGE

Edited by
LISA BING
Edited by
THERESA SCHULTZ

May Sage © 2017

ISBN-13: 978-0995667686
ISBN-10: 0995667683

VISIONS

*C*oveney, on your left!

Hearing his Alpha's warning, the Head Enforcer of the Wyvern Pride turned just in time to block the jaw of the wolf, preventing him from aiming for his neck, but the shifter still bit his flank pretty hard and deep.

They were outnumbered, practically six to one - seven felines against three dozen wolves - but seeing his wound, Rye still ordered Coveney to get back to their pride house.

I can still help, the tiger said through the pride link.

He probably could, but at what price? The gash needed to be bound, or he'd bleed out at the entrance of their territory.

In other circumstances, Ola could have healed him, at

least partially, but the lioness was currently relentlessly fighting against three females. Stopping to heal him right now was the equivalent of asking for a break, so she could make a cup of tea and eat muffins.

Go help Jas, Rygan replied, referring to their strongest female.

Jas hadn't been happy about it, but she'd stayed behind, with the non-fighters and the children. She was too far for Rye to get a good reading on her through the pride link, but he sensed some distress, which meant that some wolves had made it past their lines of defense.

Fuck.

Coveney didn't protest, presumably feeling the same call coming from the rest of their pride. Blood trailing him, he ran towards their homes.

Satisfied his Head Enforcer wasn't in imminent danger anymore, Rye grabbed the wolf on his back by the scruff of his neck, his long fangs breaking the skin, and threw him at the nearest wall. He jumped on the one standing in front of him, claws digging in its back before his teeth closed on the wolf's face. Now those were taken care of, he turned to Tracy. Ola was dealing with more opponents but Tracy was younger, and more vulnerable. His claws hooked on the flanks of one of the wolves attacking her, and tore through him.

Taking a second to observe their progress, he saw that his pride wasn't nearly as outnumbered now. Rye had incapacitated at least ten wolves, but the real hero was Daunte, his crazy-ass Beta: the humongous, graceful panther was killing a wolf every other second. The others weren't doing badly either.

They were winning.

Until they lost everything.

In the distance, Coveney roared, a gut-clenching sound that made them all stop and turn in the direction of their home. With some effort, Rye managed to push through the pride link, despite the five miles separating them, and asked his Enforcer, *What is it?*

Coveney shared what his eyes saw.

Fire. Their house was burning, each door and window reinforced, barricaded. No scream came from within.

Their pride members were already all dead.

COVENEY CURSED LIKE A SAILOR, while Daunte punched the wall, enraged, sick to his stomach. The younglings in their pride, their submissive…they were all dead.

The only thing keeping them sane right now was the fact that it hadn't happened. Yet. They were all gathered in the common room of their pride house, and

4 | MAY SAGE

there was no wolf in sight. But what they'd all seen would happen, if they didn't change the course of their actions.

Blessing the day when their Seer had joined them, as he often did, Rye closed his eyes, tuning out his pride-mates' distress and trying to concentrate on finding a solution.

They didn't have a lot of time; whenever Hsu had a vision, they needed to move their asses and act fast, if they wanted to avoid the outcome she'd foreseen. They'd ignored her once - because who would believe the word of a six year old child no one knew a thing about? - and they'd paid for it in blood.

Never again. Three years had passed since, and the child had saved their skins so often it was almost embarrassing.

"Can you concentrate for me, puppet?" he gently asked her.

It was a heavy burden to place on a child's shoulders but what choice did they have?

Hsu nodded, and took his hand.

He ran through solutions; attacking first, blocking their gates, moving the pride, keeping some fighters behind...

No, no, no, and definitely not. Hsu shared her visions with him as he thought of different paths, and all he saw was more fire. Blood. He could even smell it, which meant that their little Seer was getting stronger.

Another issue for another time.

Suddenly, the child's head snapped left, and she smiled - a rare occurrence. The kid was normally almost as serious as Rye.

"That will work," she said, talking to Daunte.

Rye turned to his Beta, giving the man all his attention, but instead of merrily telling them all about his idea, the man seemed like a deer caught in headlights, shifting uncomfortably from one foot to the next, and remaining silent.

Interesting. Daunte was normally an open book, and as Alpha, Rye had no issue reading him through the pride link. He couldn't get his actual thoughts, but he got his cat's feelings. Right now, the usually playful, easygoing animal was snarling at the Alpha, warning him to stay away.

Rye was surprised, and slightly miffed, but there wasn't much he could do about it. When he'd formed his pride, he'd made it clear that he intended to run it fairly; his pridemates were entitled to their private shit, unless they were on trial.

Instead of pushing, as his instincts wanted him to, he asked, "What is it?"

"That was just a wayward thought. There's... There's

somewhere safe. But the territory is claimed, and we wouldn't be welcome there."

He was hiding something, and again, the animal inside Rye rushed to the surface, urging him to push harder. Rye told his furry counterpart to shut it. Firstly, it wasn't the way he ran his pride, secondly, there was a very, very good chance that Daunte would push back, and no one wanted that.

The Beta was one of the strongest dominant feline shifters he'd ever met, and he could have been Alpha of his own pack if he'd wanted. Rye could take him, but a confrontation between them wouldn't be pretty.

"Hsu thinks it will work."

"It might," Daunte admitted. "But going there would mean I'd have to break my word, and lose a friend's trust. Let's run through other possibilities."

Rye let it go, and they spent the next two hours thinking about a way to win their conflict with the pack of wolves who attacked them everywhere they went.

Fire. Blood. Water. Silver.

Hsu was white, weak, and holding back her tears after replaying the death of her friends over and over again; she also always became more agitated as the moment when her visions would come to pass drew nearer. Hsu never could tell when a prediction would occur, but the weather, and the age of the kids was a good indication; little Lola, their toddler, didn't appear to be older at all in the visions, which meant that they were running out of time.

Rye was about to command Daunte to sort his shit out, but the Beta didn't need him to say anything.

"Enough!" Daunte yelled, holding his hands up in surrender. "Enough. We'll go. She'll just have to deal with it."

"She?" Rye asked, crocking an eyebrow.

Daunte sighed.

"The territory I thought about belongs to a loner no one in their right mind would cross. She *may* let us stay temporarily. If I ask nicely. After she kicks my ass."

Daunte didn't appear to be joking, which was intriguing. Female cat shifters were strong, fast, sneaky, and some could take a male in combat, although males were generally larger, more muscular. But his Beta was *Daunte Cross*, son of The Butcher, an actual feral shifter, with a reputation for chopping off heads more often than he spoke. He'd taught Daunte well, which made him one of the only males who came close to Rye's level of strength and dominance.

But the Beta genuinely seemed to think that the female he spoke of *could* beat him.

"I only have one request. Let me deal with her. Whatever she does to me, don't intervene."

Ah. So, Daunte had a thing for the woman. That explained a lot.

"Consider it done."

Moving was never pleasant but they were used to it; even the kids helped packing their belongings.

Rye didn't have a lot of stuff; he shoved his clothes in two suitcases, and that was him done. Before going downstairs to help the others, he sighed, and grabbed his phone to do what he had to do.

"Hello."

The phone call was unavoidable. If his family learned that he'd moved without telling them, he was in for a world of drama and guilt trips.

"Rygan," his brother replied on the other end of the line, calling him by his full name.

"Colter."

"I take it this isn't a courtesy call."

It never was. They weren't the warm and fuzzy kind.

"We'll be moving to Oregon tomorrow. I thought mother would want to know."

They both knew it was their overbearing, controlling father who would have caused drama if he hadn't informed him - although Rye was the Alpha of his own pack, his dad was still acting like he was under his thumb.

"Right. Hang on."

The sound was muted on the other end of the phone for a few minutes, and then Colter was back online.

"Give us an address when you arrive. Dad says you can take his jet."

Rye had to admit, tiring as family matters were, they had their perks.

FIRST SIGHT

*R*ygan let his tiger run free at dawn, hoping to feel more settled afterwards, but the animal was on edge. Unusual. The beast he shifted into was, for a lack of better word, a complete dork. It would have been happy spending all of eternity in a box, with a rope toy and a few trees nearby. His priorities were simple, straightforward- protecting his pack, playing. Not necessarily in that order.

Today, the tiger wasn't interested in a run, or a dip in their pool. It wanted to get on the road, so Rygan shifted back and went to help, in order to speed up their departure.

Twelve hours later, he still wasn't in the best of moods, all of his protective instincts working overtime as he was separated from the most vulnerable members of his pride. He really didn't like the plan they'd come up with. Following them wouldn't be hard; they'd left a trail a mile wide.

He got Coveney to fly with Ola, Tracy, Kim and the seven cubs they'd adopted into their fold; although Niamh would probably take offense to being called that. Since she'd turned twelve, the little girl had tried to grow up too fast, not caring about the fact that her lipstick and high heels were turning his hair prematurely gray. There he was, thirty-one, going on eighty-one thanks to the millions of duties falling on his shoulders. Being the Alpha of a pride was no joke.

Flying wasn't too much of an issue - using his father's jet meant that the wolves wouldn't be able to track their details, like they would have if they'd taken a commercial transit. But the rest of them weren't as discreet. Christine, their only submissive, was traveling on the back of his motorcycle; Daunte and Ian flanked his sides, while Jas drove a SUV with their belongings behind them.

He would have breathed easier if they'd made a detour to get any follower off their trail, but Daunte was adamant that they needed to arrive before the kids, so that they might settle things with the mysterious loner.

Every passing minute, Rygan was more intrigued about the woman who made his Beta stress out so much.

"Chill," he told him at their last pit stop before they'd

made it to the place Daunte had input into their GPSs. "If you can't sweet talk her, we can pay her off."

They might not be the biggest, oldest, or the most fearful pride out there, but they certainly didn't lack funds.

Rygan had been given a fair bit of cash by his grandmother when he'd become Alpha, and he'd invested it wisely. Besides, unlike a lot of shifters out there - they normally kept to themselves, finding roles within their community, and shutting out the rest of the world - most of the members of the pride had businesses.

Christine handcrafted some girly shit that somehow sold - hats, scarves, Teddy Bears and god knew what - Coveney was a wiz behind a computer and pimped his skills as a PI, Jas had a popular travel blog, Ian invested in start-ups, Tracy wrote novels. Rygan didn't demand it but they all pitched in, dropping some of their profit in the pride's savings account when they could. Which was often. Last time he'd looked, the amount in their savings had a lot of zeros. No loner was going to turn up her nose at the kind of bribes they could afford.

But, surprising and intriguing him again, Daunte snorted, "No. Trust me, if she doesn't want us in her territory, there's nothing we can say or do to change her mind."

Daunte was adamant, but he didn't elaborate, to Rye's annoyance.

They finished the last leg of their journey within the next couple of hours; by the time they stopped in front of a handsome plantation built at the heart of a wild, untamed forest, Rye was imagining that they would be met by a she-bear, a fearsome witch, or maybe even a damn vampire.

"Wow. This place is beautiful."

It was; the location, the old house with ivy crawling up the walls, and those strong, high trees surrounding it were picturesque. His cat was seriously drooling over the untamed landscape, desperate to shift. He wanted to go play. Badly. But now wasn't the time, and Rygan told him so.

Quiet.

The tiger inside him was normally more or less amenable - he understood that Rye let him have its say when he could - but today, it felt agitated. There was... something. He couldn't place his finger on it. He scented something that made every part of him uneasy, unhinged.

Rye had no gift, but there was a fair bit of witch blood in his family tree - his grandmother had healing powers, like Ola, his aunt was a Seer, and his mother, a powerful empath - and he knew that meant he should listen to his instincts more than the average shifter so, he stayed vigilant, ready for the world to explode.

"Do I hear a waterfall?" Ian asked, and Daunte pointed west.

"Yep, that way. There's a lake further into the forest, too."

Ola shook her head and playfully bumped his shoulder.

"You're in deep shit for not telling us about this place before. It's perfect."

They'd moved seven times over the last ten years, since he'd formed the pride, but they'd never settled anywhere nearly as nice; these kinds of places were normally packed with humans, but during their ride over, they hadn't come across even one house. This was the perfect location for a pride.

"Oh, he most certainly is in deep shit."

They all tensed and turned away from the view and towards the direction of the beautiful, singsong voice, startled because none of them had felt or heard anyone approach, even though Rye had been on high alert.

Fuck.

Rygan had a hard time staying focused; the moment he saw her, his entire attention was captured by her.

The brunette who'd appeared on the step of the

elegant home was small, petite, delicate, and dangerous. Her aura said so. The way she moved said so.
The way his tiger clawed to the surface, urging Rygan
forward, *definitely* said so.

His tiger had never paid any attention to a female
before. *Never.* He didn't form any words, but Rygan
understood his feeling completely. Usually, when
Rygan looked at women he found appealing, his
animal was bored, finding them unworthy of his attention. Pitiful. Weak. He told him, *play with it if you must,
but don't get me involved.* Problematic, as no shifter could
hope to form a relationship if their animal didn't
approve.

Right now the dumb tiger, who should have bared his
teeth, jumped and said *chase the pretty kitty.*

Shit.

Daunte echoed his curse, holding his hands up, "Look,
I can explain."

He actually didn't finish the last word, as her foot was
kicking him ten feet back. The woman had effortlessly
jumped to him, and she did it again, one of her knees
colliding with his jaw, while the other wrapped around
his neck. She did a flip that turned his Beta flat on the
ground, all in a few seconds.

Jas was stepping forward, ready to defend her pride-
mate, but Rygan held her back. Normally, because of
their difference in size and muscle mass, females

fought females and males fought males, so it was understandable that the enforcer felt like intervening; but Daunte wasn't letting the woman win out of courtesy. He was trying to push her, struggling to get up. She'd just beat his ass, fair and square, without breaking a sweat.

What. The. Hell.

"He told us to stay back," Rygan reminded Jas, and the woman's head snapped to his.

She'd caught his tiger's attention immediately, but now she had his.

Damn. She was a fucking wet dream. Those fiery golden eyes turned cat - narrow irises and all - that pretty face, and every sinful curve her yoga pants and t-shirt weren't hiding got him hard; almost as much as her display of dominance.

She narrowed her eyes as her gaze crossed his, and he couldn't exactly place a word on what transpired there. He only knew one thing: she was hot. Very, very hot. He wanted her so bad it was almost painful.

Cutting their staring contest short, her head snapped back to Daunte, making Rye want to roar in protest. He'd never been so easily dismissed. Most females, dominant or not, would have nodded to him, at least.

He didn't like her indifference to his status or his vibes. Not. One. Bit. His tiger heartily disagreed, seeing it as a challenge.

"You told them to leave us alone? Wise," she sweetly said to his Beta, "What else did you say about me?"

Her knee dug harder into his Beta's throat, and Daunte croaked, "Nothing, I swear. Dammit Aisling, I didn't have a choice. We have cubs. A witch, a Seer, and five others. One of them is two."

While she kept Daunte on the ground for another ten seconds, she then got up, letting him go.

"Talk."

"Wolves. We fight them, but some of them stay back, and aim for the weaker members of the pack. They never make it. Our Seer's just nine, but she's gotten stronger and stronger over the last three years - what she sees happens unless we change our decisions. I just thought for one second that we could stay here for a while, and she saw we were safe if we did that. Do you really think I would have come to you if I had any other choice? I don't actually enjoy getting my ass kicked."

The woman glared, but the glow of her eyes slowly faded; they reverted back to her natural human gaze, an amber which was a little more normal, and just as mesmerizing.

"You could have called," she grumbled, turning back towards the house without another word.

Rye looked - of course he looked. Fuck, she could walk away from him any day, with an ass like that.

Daunte got to his feet, and smiled, yelling after her, "We'll be here a week, tops - downstairs, no one will go upstairs. Then, we'll get a place nearby. We'll stay out of your way."

He wasn't asking permission, and to everyone's surprise, the woman he'd called Aisling just shrugged indifferently.

"You still run that bakery?" he asked, and somehow that must have been pushing his luck, because she turned, her eyes flashing gold again.

"We'll order in bulk. Delivery. The entire pride will completely stay out of your way. That's a promise."

She turned again, and walk away, replying, "I'll over-charge you."

Daunte yelled back a, "Love you!" that earned him a growl.

Rygan wasn't quite certain what had occurred, and apparently, he wasn't the only one because Jas asked, "So, we have a place to stay?"

Daunte turned to her and winked.

"Yep. And more surprisingly, I still have my balls."

SANCTUARY

*T*he house was completely unexpected inside. The decor had been kept minimalistic, save for the cat furniture running along the walls and ceiling. Trees, ramps, elegant toys fixed to the wall.

Aisling was apparently the ultimate crazy cat lady, which was yet another thing to add to the ever growing list of What The Fuck about her. Shifters didn't often keep pets, as domestic animals felt intimidated and weirded out by them, but there was at least half a dozen different cats in the house.

Rygan frowned. Most doors and windows were opened, letting them roam free. Obviously, the woman wasn't wary of intruders. Finding himself assessing the house, he inwardly shook his head, concerned about her safety, and pissed at her for not taking it into consideration. Sure, she obviously could take care of herself, but that didn't mean that she should be quite so careless; a burglar didn't even need to break in as things were - he could just casually waltz inside. What if she was out of it when a criminal got in? Drunk, or napping. Most felines weren't known for being light sleepers.

His protective instincts were working overtime, which was *normal*. Or so he told himself. Alphas were naturally prone to worrying, especially when half of their pride wasn't in the vicinity.

Yep. Rygan was fully aware that he was bullshitting himself. While the statement was true, his protective instincts were only triggered by children, unprotected submissives and his own pride members. In short, he shouldn't give a fuck about Aisling, the stranger, the loner. And he was surprised, and weirded out by the fact that, for some reason, he did.

"Is that a lynx?"

They all froze; if shifters could spook domestic cats, they completely freaked wild ones. Many shifters had been mauled by animals, in part because they always felt so reluctant about antagonizing what their cats saw as their less fortunate peers, dumber but endearing versions of themselves.

The feline, which was indeed a lynx, snarled in Rygan's direction before running along a rope bridge leading from one wall to the next, and got out of doors as fast as he could.

"Ace runs a feline sanctuary," Daunte explained.

Ace. It suited her. Why did it piss him off that he had a nickname for the woman?

"She normally gets wounded animals back on their feet, and takes them back to the wild, but I'm pretty sure I saw that grumpy puss here last year," he said, sounding surprised.

Then, he gave them a grand tour of the ground floor, visibly familiar with the house. The bedrooms were large, pleasing, and prepared for visitors.

"Kitchen, bathroom, second bathroom, bedroom-we'll have to share, there's only three downstairs."

It didn't really bother him; they'd slept in two rooms before - the kids and the women together, and the guys had bunked together in a lounge - but he found his eyes glaring at the ceiling. Did the woman really have to keep the whole upper floor to herself?

But then again, if he asked himself what would have happened had an unknown pride turned up at his door without warning, he had to sigh and concede that the woman wasn't exactly being difficult. Still. He and his tiger, in perfect agreement, for the first time today, would have preferred to sleep closer to her.

Much closer.

"Rye, you take this one," he said, pointing to the smallest of the three rooms. "The rest of us can manage."

He didn't mind the small room at all, but he still frowned.

"Why did you say we'd stay downstairs? The house is large and the rest of you will be crowded."

"We don't want to piss Aisling off. Trust me on that. We're already abusing her hospitality."

Rygan glared at his friend, pissed that he felt like punching his throat. He wasn't possessive of the females he took to his bed, he wasn't even particularly protective of the females in his pride, beyond a basic need to know they were well. He *shouldn't* want to inflict damage on one of his closest pridemates.

"How come I've never heard of her?" he asked - or demanded to know. "Dammit, Daunte, I've known you for sixteen years."

They had first crossed paths at a Fest Daunte had attended with his mother. The feline prides around the continent kept a low profile, because of their constant wars with wolves. They weren't frightened, but contrary to lupine packs, feline prides put the safety of their cubs above all else. Wolves had too much pride and not enough sense to think about their children when they attacked; wild cats did. But every year, the leader of all feline Alphas called a meeting, for various reasons; the Alphas, Betas and Enforcers saw it as work, but for the rest of the gathering, it was just a humongous party. Barbecue, friendly competitions, and - he learned when he was a little older - orgies, too.

Daunte had been surly, too serious for a ten year old kid and his pridemates had seemed to make fun of him. Rye hadn't been the most sociable of sixteen year olds at the time, but on an impulse, he decided to talk to him; because of his status, singling him out warned the bullies away.

He never would have guessed he was talking to The Butcher's son. He never would have guessed he'd earn his loyalty so easily; but he did. The moment he turned eighteen, Daunte requested a transfer to Rygan's pride, although at the time, it had been ridiculously tiny, and threatened on every front.

As he'd met the guy every year for the first eight years of their acquaintance, and then, had been his Alpha for the next eight, he was surprised, and irritated that he knew nothing about a woman he was visibly…familiar with.

He was sticking to that reason, although the beast inside him had a much simpler explanation. The usually simple, playful tiger bared his fangs and growled at their friend. *Stay away from her,* it said. *Mine.*

"Aisling and I go way back," Daunte replied.

That wasn't even the beginning of the start of a vague sort of response, and Ian, who was shamelessly eavesdropping, snorted at that.

"And you went to see her less than a year ago…"

"I didn't actually hide my vacation, Rye. You know I went away last July. You didn't ask where."

Rygan just glared.

"What?"

"You're hiding things - from *us*. Your pride."

"I'm not hiding anything relevant about the pride, or about me. I get that you're curious - I would be too. But Aisling is a close friend of mine - someone I've known for longer than any of you. And she wants her shit to stay private. You know better than to think I'll betray my friend's confidence."

Yes. Unfortunately, they did know better. Daunte kept his words, hence why he had been so conflicted about leading them here; if he'd promised Aisling he wouldn't, it had gone against everything he was. Rye should be thanking his Beta for putting the safety of the pride above all else - even above his honor.

Being perfectly conscious of all that didn't stop him from glaring at Daunte, making his displeasure clear without pushing his dominant vibes to attempt to force his will on him. His Beta didn't look away.

The rest of the pride arrived then, just in time to break their stare off. Rygan's priority was always his pride; he turned to the door, checked that everyone was here.

"How was the flight?" he asked his Head Enforcer.

It was a tall, willowy blonde who answered, cutting off Coveney.

"Horrid," Kim told him, her whiny voice annoying as always. "The flight attendants were rude, and your dad should fire the damn pilot. You wouldn't believe how unsteady we were, I thought we were going to crash."

Rygan ignored the dominant female, as he usually did. He didn't think she was able to describe anything without finding cause to complain. He would never have accepted her in the pride, if she hadn't been Jas' twin.

Jas and her sister had been loners since their childhood - or rather, they simply hadn't lived with a pride, but they'd had a home. They had been adopted by humans. From what Rye knew of it, Jas had been a daddy's girl, and her military trained father had taught her everything he knew, while their mother had given all of her attention to Kim, taking her shopping, getting her nose and tits done when she'd asked for it. Although they had been identical once, the two women couldn't look more different now. Jas wore her dark hair short, cut like a pixie's; her little turned up nose and her pouty mouth made people mistakenly think she was sweet. Kim was all for the long, blonde, straight Barbie look, and she was still waiting for her Ken. Rye didn't often pay attention to what she said, but from what he'd unfortunately overheard over the years, she fully intended to marry well - only an Alpha or a billionaire would do.

They'd joined the pride because their parents had said they should give it a try - being loners meant that shifters around them had treated them like crap. Men expected them to be for sale, women mistrusted them. Jas had turned up one day, and explained her predicament.

"We have money, so we won't use your resources." She'd also been completely sincere when she'd added, "My sister will be a burden, but I'll make up for it."

Rygan immediately took to Jas, he loved how straightforward she was. If his tiger had showed any interest, he might even have asked her out. As for Kim… everyone sighed when she walked in, wearing stilettos and a non-existent skirt.

But her endless, generally barely covered legs probably had something to do with the reason why he hadn't protested when she'd asked to join. He had just been twenty-two at the time, after all.

"IT WENT OKAY," Coveney translated. "There was some turbulence for ten minutes. Your dad sent one of his drivers, so we didn't need to rent a car."

He nodded, reassured. That meant that there was no paper trail of their whereabouts; if they created a false trail quickly enough, they might manage to stay inconspicuous a little longer.

He wasn't delusional enough to think that the wolves would just abandon their relentless hunt - they'd find them eventually. But at least, the pride had some time to work things out - time they desperately needed.

Until now, Rygan had assumed that the wolves were hunting them on principle; his status meant that beating his pride would give any wolf an extra dose of street cred. But what they'd seen in Hsu's vision? Attacking kids and submissives? Feline or wolf, there was no honor in it.

Rygan needed to work out their enemy's motivation, and find a way to really get them off their backs, before it was too late.

"Let's get the kids settled - only unload the essentials, we'll be leaving as soon as possible. Once that's done, we need to call our contacts and get to the bottom of things. The way we're getting hunted is personal. Time to find out why."

FAMILY

*C*atching a familiar scent, Ace lifted her head, and called Clary from the back of her small bakery.

"Hey sweet. Do you mind taking over at the counter? It's pretty quiet."

Clarissa had been her assistant since she'd come back from college, six months prior, although she had an MBA, there weren't a ton of exciting jobs in Lakesides.

In many a place, some would have frowned at a human working in a bakery owned by a shifter, but Ace had struck gold with this town.

It wasn't that the people of Lakesides *liked* shifters - they were human, so most of them didn't, understandably finding them scary as fuck - but before her, they'd dealt with a guy who pillaged, raped, and murdered, so they'd learned to appreciate her perhaps overly sarcastic, but otherwise charming self.

Well, maybe not *charming*, but she didn't have murderous tendencies most of the time.

THE TOWNSPEOPLE HAD REPORTED the pack terrorizing them, but human authorities couldn't do much - they just told the shifter council, who'd demanded that the wolves fixed the issue. Only, wolves weren't organized the way feline shifters were.

Felines had a leader, a governing body, so to speak. They may not be officially recognized in the US, but they called their leader their King, and he was just that. If someone went out of line, they had the authorities in place to take care of it - so no feline messed up.

Wolves had a Head Pack, and when it wanted to act, it was lethal. However, that pack only moved its finger when someone directly threatened *them*. The rest, they shrugged off, putting it on their To Do list for a decade or two. Aisling was sure that eventually, they would have come to take care of the issue, but they left it for over a year.

Aisling pitied their race. Not all of them were bad; in fact, most wolves weren't, but their authority was so corrupted, they couldn't do a thing about their reputation. That was the reason why there were more loner wolves than any other kind of shifter out there; in general, those who'd left their pack had a damn good reason to have chosen that lifestyle. Aisling's cat suffered from the isolation, but not nearly as much as a wolf ever would. Their species, like their animal counterpart, was really meant to live in groups.

It was a wolf who'd told her about Lakesides; her friend, Vivicia, had just mentioned it in passing, unknowingly planting a seed. Ace had lived in Los Angeles, and damn if the city of Angels wasn't all about drama. Although they paid well, she'd been tired of having to deal with the angel, nephilim, and demon issues there. She'd been ready to find somewhere to settle down at the time, and somewhere so isolated a pack could get away with murder - literally - was her idea of perfection, so she'd turned up in town, to see it for herself. People had been pretty mistrusting, but after a couple of pints at the local bar, they'd felt protective enough to tell her to pack her things and go before the Alpha wolf living near heard of her being there.

They'd really feared the man, that much had been obvious. Ace wasn't sure whether she would have chosen to stay - after living in the city for seven years, Lakesides had seemed awfully small - but the day after she'd arrived, the stupid-ass Alpha had showed his face at her hotel, demanding *favors* for letting her live.

Yeah, that had gone down well. She slit his throat and cut his balls off.

The humans had been grateful at first, but wary, with good reasons; as she could so easily dispose of a man so huge, dominant, and subdue his entire pack with her vibes, they'd wondered if they'd been thrown out of the pan and right into the fire. So, she kept a low profile, turned up on game day to watch football at the pub. Bored out of her mind, she bought an empty store and did it up. She didn't exactly have a *thing*, a passion, like some did. She loved reading, running, knitting, swimming, and if she was entirely honest with herself, she kind of liked fighting too. But while nothing made her feel excited, there was one activity that soothed her mind, making her reach that special place- home.

Baking.

A long, long time ago, a sweet female shifter who always hummed, or sang, had popped her on top of the kitchen countertop as she rolled dough; later, she got her to help. Baking was home. Every time she smelled apple pies cooking in her oven, she remembered the little piece of happiness the woman had carved for her.

So, she opened a bakery. She wasn't classically trained, but apparently, her things were good enough for the people of Lakesides. Ace was certain that what had nailed the deal had been her cupcakes. Which, by the way, were pretty awesome.

Three years later, it was the mayor who'd approached Ace, asking if she could use an employee when Clarissa had come back to town. Ace, who was pulling fifteen hour shifts between baking, serving customers and delivering orders, jumped on it and hadn't had any reason to regret it since.

"Sure, take as much time as you need," the ever enthusiastic, ever smiling woman replied.

She thanked her and headed to her kitchen, following her nose.

Suddenly, a hand closed over her lips and a pair of strong arms pulled her in a dark corner of her shop. A smile played on her lips. In other circumstances, she might already have drop kicked her attacker. As soon as they were locked in a cupboard, her kidnapper's arms went around her waist, engulfing her in a bear hug. She let him.

Ace wasn't touchy-feely but she was a shifter - a *cat* shifter. That kind of contact was a balm to her soul when it came from the right person. Daunte Cross was one of the few people whose touch she accepted.

He chuckled, his annoyingly huge chest moving against her cheek. As much as she'd like to pretend otherwise, he was all man now.

"Hey sis," he whispered.

He liked to call her that in private; because she didn't let him say it in public. Not anymore. She'd shed the name Cross and all its meaning long ago.

She pushed his chest back and glared up - and up, and up. The boy was tall, damn him.

"Did you by any chance lose my number? You know, the one I had you memorize at nine years old?"

Daunte never played fair; he pouted and his big amber eyes went all pleading and cute.

"I can't do that expression over the phone. You would totally have told me to take a hike."

The man had a point. Dammit.

She sighed and climbed on top of a shelf, asking, "Okay what's the deal?"

It really wasn't her problem; they even had an agreement - whenever they'd met up over the years, they never spoke of the issues they encountered in their lives. Being siblings didn't give them the right to be in each other's business.

But he'd changed the rules of the game by turning up; she needed to know what sort of mess he'd brought to her doorstep.

"We don't know. Our pride was always in danger - from felines who think one of our enforcers is a criminal, although he was acquitted, and from shifters around us, because we're small and they assume it makes us easy pickings. But that pack... they've been on our case for about two, three years, wherever we go. We stayed where we were, and fought them whenever they came to our door, at first, but then, they went after one of our kids - a sixteen year old, while he was at school. He didn't make it."

Daunte's eyes were cold, and for a minute he reminded her of their father.

"We're strong, Ace. All of us. But we're ten adults, and there's seven kids. We have no clue who they are, honestly, but every time they attack us, they completely outnumber us. There're at least sixty fighters in their pack - I'm sure they have kids who would make them vulnerable too, but we'd never target them anyway."

She nodded, understanding. But that didn't change a fact.

"I'm happy here, Daunte. No one bothers me. You know I've never turned away any loner who needed to lie low, but an entire pride? That *will* bring some attention to my territory."

And it was just that: hers. She'd stuck to the location after killing the Alpha for one simple reason: she had been able to buy the entire forest, its lake, its mountains, and the twelve houses built on it. The pack of wolves who'd lived there before her had just rented; the territory had belonged to an old family who'd been more than happy to sell out to her, because they'd known she wouldn't pull any shit on them.

Having a pride settled in town might damage the little piece of home she'd managed to carve for herself.

"I know," Daunte replied, nodding. "But the pride is family, and I do whatever I can to protect my family. If it means begging my big sister for help? So be it."

She rolled her eyes, but her expression was still guarded.

"What?"

Ace took a few seconds, deciding whether she really wanted to bring up the subject. Then, she gave into what her cat was demanding - what she herself really wanted to know.

"Your Alpha. I need you to tell me about your Alpha."

Need was a strong word; she needed water, fresh air and cupcakes. Information about a complete stranger shouldn't have seemed as essential to her - but it was.

The man had made *quite* the impression on her, and she would feel off balance until she could pinpoint why.

CLUELESS

They were settled by dusk - Daunte had taken a trip to a nearby store to stock up on supplies they might need, Ian and Jas got the three rooms set up, and most of the others unpacked while Christine took care of the kids.

Kim painted her nails. Then, she watched them dry.

As well as the expected essentials, Daunte came back with a heavy tray containing doughnuts, cupcakes, chocolate cakes and mini pies. Rygan narrowed his eyes, catching something else over the scent of sugar, butter and vanilla. Something woodsy and spicy.

"Your friend Aisling made these?" he guessed, grabbing a miniature apple pie.

Daunte nodded, sharing the goodies around.

Hell. This was a *good* pie. He peeked into the box his Beta had left on the dining room table, and found a cupcake left in there. Rygan had just grabbed it when he sensed someone looking at him; he turned to find Hsu staring at him with watery eyes, like he'd just kicked his way through an entire litter of puppies.

He sighed and regretfully put the cupcake in her little hands, ruffling her hair, although the kid was nothing short of a damn manipulative cupcake thief.

"Try that in ten years," he said, his tone warning her.

She giggled and merrily skipped away.

As Daunte was back, and the pack had had a second to relax, Rygan started to get organized.

"Coveney," he said, calling his Head Enforcer, "Check the perimeter, we need to make sure it's safe. Let me know if you catch any suspicious scents. Then, come back and start digging up what you can about those wolves." His proficiency with a computer made him the best person for the job, although it wasn't the first time they'd looked. They just didn't have enough information to know where to start. "And Jas," Rygan stopped himself, feeling uneasy about sending her away so soon after she'd arrived. But he put the safety of his pride before anything else, and Jas was his best tracker. Her upbringing also made her navigate the world with ease, passing for a human if she wanted to. The rest of them never quite shook off their wildness, their otherness.

"I'll be out there at dawn," she said before he added anything else, knowing exactly what he'd demand of her. "You want me to locate the members of the wolf pack, set up a false trail, and fish for information."

Rygan nodded, and breathed a little better now they had an immediate plan of action. He wouldn't completely relax until they had answers, though. What did those wolves have against them?

ON ANOTHER FRONT, Rygan felt just as frustrated. Since their arrival the previous day, they kept Daunte's word and stayed out of their elusive host's way, even though, honestly, it *killed* him.

They were all curious by nature, but Rygan was also not used to being told no, so dangling a sexy feline shifter wrapped in mystery, and saying that he couldn't ask questions about her, was the equivalent of waving a humongous flag in front of a bull on steroids.

Daunte stayed mostly silent although, and despite his little speech, the questions poured from every side, some more obvious than others. He only revealed what must have been common knowledge - impersonal facts. They knew Aisling was a loner, they knew she'd lived in this home for three years, and that they were allowed to borrow her milk if they replaced it; but he said nothing when they asked where she came from, which pride she used to belong to - even her last name wasn't something he was willing to divulge.

Dick.

"This place is freaking awesome," Ian told them, coming back from a run. "And it *looks* made for a pride - or a pack. This house might be the first one anyone traveling through the forest by car will come across, but there are others, further into the woods."

The annoying Beta nodded, "That's right. There was a pack of wolves settled here, before. They were bad news and the humans in the nearby town were pretty worried. Ace took over; she gets along pretty well with the towners. Owns her bakery there and all."

Rygan openly snorted at that, making everyone look at him with a questioning expression; probably because he wasn't the kind of man who snorted. Ever. He just said what he had in mind, and moved on, preferring to keep things simple, straightforward.

What the hell was wrong with him?

"What?"

"You're saying that a lone female singlehandedly took on a pack of wolves?"

"I never said she did it by herself - Aisling has plenty of contacts, and she could have called them," Daunte replied, rolling his eyes. "But in this case, she didn't need them. She challenged the Alpha and got it over with."

Another snort.

Yes. He was being an asshole. He was questioning what he'd seen with his own eyes the previous night: Aisling had taken Daunte without any issue and Rygan knew his Beta was more dominant, and better trained that most Alphas. But asking questions hadn't worked and Rygan wasn't beyond fishing for information instead.

"An Alpha wolf, really? She's a tiny thing. You went easy on her yesterday, didn't you?"

He knew Daunte hadn't, but predictably, he narrowed his eyes and grew defensive.

"Going easy on Ace is nothing short of suicide. Forget whatever you think you know about females. She's stronger than me, more cunning than Coveney, faster than you…and not very fond of being insulted. You might want to prevent yourself from doing so in her house."

Rygan flipped Daunte off, before taking a seat on one of the sofas; immediately, the little girl playing on the floor, their youngest, grabbed her toy and climbed on his lap.

"Hey Lola Bear," he said, some of his dreadful humor disappearing as the kitten beamed at him.

Try as the others might, he remained that girl's favorite, which meant she'd probably grow up to either be extremely dominant, or extremely submissive.

They'd found her on their doorstep one day, without

so much as a letter of explanation. The kid had just been a few days old at the time. Rygan guessed someone had heard that his pride took on kids, and chosen to give them the newborn. Probably a lone female, or someone in danger. They could smell that she was a feline shifter, but at her age, it was hard to tell which kind. They wouldn't know for sure until she shifted, probably at puberty. It didn't matter; various members of the prides were of different breeds - one of them wasn't a shifter at all - but they all claimed each other. Lola was theirs now, just like Hsu, Jasper, Clive, Victoria, Daniel, Will and Niamh. Some thought having so many kids made their pride weak; and in a way, they were right. They were vulnerable. But there was also strength in having something to fight for.

"Did you have fun in the plane?"

She proceeded to babble about her journey, using actual words mixed with gibberish, but entertaining as the child was, his attention was soon diverted.

He felt like someone watched him, and lifting his gaze, it landed on one of the elegant cat trees fixed on the walls.

After their arrival, the animals they'd met the first day had all gone out of doors, preferring to stay in the backyard or the nearby trees, but, calmly lounging on top of the highest piece of furniture, there was one cat left.

Rygan smiled. He didn't often do so, but right now, he couldn't help it. The animal was endearing, curled up on its back, stretching languorously. It was one of the fancy pets humans had bred to entertain themselves; something wild mixed with a domestic race.

"Is that a Bengal?" he asked Ian.

Cat shifters knew most breeds of wild cats out there, but they didn't usually have a keen interest in domestic cats; Ian, however, was the annoying know it all of their group, and as such, he'd probably know.

The guy shook his head. "Definitely not, no. He's spotted, not marble. The markings make him look a little like a Savannah," he said, "He's bigger than a Bengal, but he's light, too. Honestly, I'm not sure. See the ears, the nose? He looks like a margay if you just concentrate on the face. I'd say, it's a mix. Beautiful, though."

Everyone stared at the pretty thing who was seemingly ignoring them from his perchoire, making a show of cleaning his claws, and Daunte laughed, correcting Ian.

"She. That's a she."

"Was she also there when you last visited?" Christine asked.

He wasn't the only one fishing for pieces of information.

"Oh yeah. That gal isn't leaving anytime soon."

"Do you know what breed she is, then?"

"Half savannah, a bit of panther, and something else. Not sure what."

"Aisling bought her, then?"

Daunte tensed. "Can we agree not to ask about Ace again? Please."

"You can't blame us," Ola told him. "We're in her house, it's nice, and we're discovering things we aren't used to. You're basically asking us to ignore all that—that's against our nature."

"No, I'm asking you to respect our host's privacy, and I'm asking you to stop hounding me."

On this note, Daunte got up, stretching.

"Right, I'm going to take a bath now so I can crash right after patrolling the perimeter later. We have a long day tomorrow."

He was avoiding the pride; everyone knew it. Rygan felt guilty that their curiosity had made the Beta feel like he couldn't chill with the rest of them. Just not guilty enough to stop fishing.

He stopped the man from leaving, though, calling him back.

"Daunte?"

The Beta didn't ignore him, but he didn't turn his heels either.

"Thank you. We're not showing it right now, but we're all grateful to you, and your friend Ace. You're saving our skin. We know it." But because he was nothing if not sincere, he added, "However, I'm not done hounding you."

LUCK

*R*ygan and Coveney sat down behind the hacker's laptop and researched rental properties in Lakesides, Oregon, expecting a big fat nothing. Their requirements were rarely met - to be comfortable, the pride needed a ten bedroom, minimum, and they also preferred homes that were fenced in. A decent territory to run around wouldn't hurt either.

As per usual, there was zero results matching their exact criteria, but before Coveney clicked away to broaden their search, Rygan stopped him, "Wait a second, what's that?"

He pointed towards an ad underneath their non-existent search results.

The main picture showed a modern home - one of those weirdly shaped buildings that seem to have been made of wooden square boxes, with large windows; Coveney clicked on it and they scrolled through pictures of elegant stairs without banisters, antique chandeliers fitted around modern lighting, plush rugs and marble countertops. The house was made to impress; the kind of things an actor might have bought.

"Fifteen rooms. There's a large garden and fences all around. It says it's just outside of town."

Clicking on the map to locate the property, Rygan felt a smile playing on his lip.

Oh dear. The pretty kitty wasn't going to like that; not one bit.

"It's just outside the forest, right?"

Rygan nodded.

"If Aisling doesn't mind, we can ask to run in her territory." Running was essential for an animal's well-being. "We can offer to patrol for her in exchange, maybe?" Coveney, sounding hopeful, turned to Daunte, who'd just walked in, his hair wet. He was wearing the dark grey clothing he liked to put on when he patrolled at night.

The Beta joined them and looked at the computer screen.

"Oh, I know that house. It was under construction last year; the mayor made it for his daughter, but she got married and moved away. Ace mentioned she might buy it."

Well, that complicated things.

"Would she rent it to us? Or let us buy it?"

Daunte grimaced, walking away, phone in hand.

"Hey lady. Look, we saw the house we talked about last time was on the market…" the Beta's voice faded as he got out, heading to the gardens. When he walked back in a few minutes later, he was smiling and nodding.

"We can buy. We can also run in her woods - as long as we stay away from her."

Rygan narrowed his eyes; it was too easy. Catching his suspicion, Daunte explained, "Ace spent a pretty penny when she moved here, between the land and her business. She *would* have bought the house, rather than letting it go to just anyone - it's too close to her territory. But she's fine with us having it. She trusts me."

That answer cleared things up, and should have made Rygan happy. It didn't. It showed too much familiarity between his Beta and the loner he had no business feeling possessive over.

WHEN THEY ANNOUNCED their find a few hours later, the response wasn't quite unanimously favorable.

"Oh," said Ola, her tone curt.

"We were going to rent, but it's too good an opportunity to pass up. We'll try to snatch that up."

Shifters liked to own their territory, but the healer still frowned, concerned.

"I thought we were only welcome here for a week? A house completion will take longer than that."

Ola, like the majority of his pride, was in a hurry to leave the strange house, so that they could protect the cubs on their own turf, but Daunte didn't feel the same need.

And nor did Rygan, if he was honest.

Overnight he'd thought about the way Ace had jumped and directly attacked. If she'd wanted, she could have drawn blood. She hadn't.

Shifters were often guilty of letting their human counterpart do all the thinking, but if he ignored it, if he wondered about her actions as a wild cat, they made sense. She'd made a point very clear: *don't fuck with me, I can take one of your strongest.*

The more Rygan thought of it, the more he was convinced that it hadn't been hostile. Not really. No pretty words could have achieved what that display did, so she'd just cut the shit. Otherwise, the dominant females in his pride might have confronted her; now, they were wary of her, happy to stay at a distance - which, Rygan assumed, was exactly what she wanted.

"Ace will let us stay," his Beta assured them. "But in exchange, the least we can do is make her some dinner. She goes to work early; if we pack some left-overs and leave it on the kitchen counter, she'll be very pleased with us."

"I'll make something nice then," Ian replied, his expression determined.

A lot of pride members cooked, Rygan included, but on special occasions, Ian took over; unfortunately, it didn't happen often. Just because the man was amazing in the kitchen didn't mean that he liked cooking.

He made a chili that had everyone shamelessly demanding seconds, and most of the pack retired for the night after finishing their food.

Rygan stayed up until the last member of his pack had gone to bed, still on edge. Things had changed too quickly for his liking; they hadn't prepared their exit, barely taking a few hours to pack their belongings. And now they depended on *her* hospitality.

If he was entirely sincere, *she* was his problem. He was wary, and with good reason. Being loners went against the nature of most shifters; it wasn't as bad for felines as it was for wolves, but they were still naturally inclined to live in prides. If she'd been cast out of hers, she'd done something really bad to deserve it. If she'd chosen to leave, it said a lot about her character - none of which was good. But at the same time, she was a friend of Daunte's. That was a recommendation on its own - he didn't think he knew one man half as loyal as the Beta. And while reason might say otherwise, his guts told Rygan he could trust Ace.

His problem with her didn't end there. The way he was drawn to her made him want to take more precautions, unsure he could trust his instincts on the matter. It was hard to tell whether he was listening to his little head or the one he should pay attention to. Perhaps he should get Coveney to run a search on her - although, without a last name, he wasn't sure they'd find much. The fact that Daunte might be pissed also made him consider it carefully. Rygan and his Beta had never really clashed about anything; he didn't want that to change. The commanding part of a pride ought to present a united front.

If he just took the facts, the answer was clear. He needed to fuck the woman, and soon. Getting it out of the way would mean he could see things with more perspective once the deed was done.

Right?

A noise pulled him out of his reverie; lifting his head, he found the object of his conflicted thoughts in the kitchen, opening her fridge.

QUESTIONS

*R*ygan frowned, wondering how the hell she'd gone past him unnoticed.

"Don't beat yourself up," the woman said without turning to him. "Not a lot of people can hear me coming."

That pissed him off; he wasn't just anyone, and he *would* have heard her, if he'd paid attention. No one snuck past him. Ever.

Although, come to think of it, it was the second time she had. He hadn't heard her approach before she'd spoken, the previous day. Ouch. His pride took a dent at that realization.

"Good evening," he said.

It hit him that these were the first words they'd ever exchanged.

Fuck. He was fascinated with the woman and they had never even *talked*. For a minute, he wondered if she could be part siren, or if she just overused some seductive potion, but as he walked towards her, her scent became stronger at each step, and what he smelled was feline, natural, and feminine. She'd just come back from a run: he could detect her usual blend of wood and spices, as well as rain and sweat. A tantalizing mixture that made him want to lick her from head to toe.

He hadn't seen her for over forty eight hours and honestly, he'd thought that his memory might have overplayed her charms - and the effect she had on him.

No such chance.

"Ace, right?"

"Daunte is one of only three people in the world who calls me Ace," she replied. "It's Aisling. At least, that doesn't make me sound like a jock."

"Aisling is a mouthful, sweetheart," he drawled. "What shall I call you?"

She rolled her eyes at that.

"Despite the admittedly noticeable southern accent, I'm not going to fall for any sort of line you could possibly come up with, so spare us both, Rygan. Call me Ace if you must. It shouldn't matter much, as you're going to stay out of my way."

He should, but he knew there was a pretty good chance he wouldn't.

"How do you know my name? I don't believe I introduced myself."

Rye wasn't particularly vain but he knew females liked what they saw. Ace was acting like he wasn't even there. But she'd asked Daunte about him, obviously, and he wanted to hear her say it, admit that she'd been curious.

"Rygan Wayland, six foot four, age thirty-one," she recited. "Second son of our good King, and Alpha of the Wyvern pride."

Grabbing a pack of raspberries and some yogurt, she closed the fridge with her foot and walked to the breakfast table.

"That puts me at a disadvantage. I know nothing about you."

Aisling tilted her head left and smirked. "That would be because only one of us happens to have a fan page."

He groaned, but conceded her point.

"It's not like I *want* one." He generally didn't find it necessary to justify anything about himself, but that damn fan page was the exception. "Coveney set up a pride website to help stay in touch with other shifters, and apparently, there was a lot of hits on my profile. He figured we might as well cash in on the traffic."

She had the decency to at least try to stifle her smile.

"And the half-naked shots?"

"Our calendar made us half a million. And it's not just *me* in it. Daunte does it, too. You'd do it, too, to feed a pride."

So, yeah, he sounded petulant as fuck.

"It's all for the greater good," she replied, nodding, but still smirking.

He didn't mind all that much; sassing or not, god knew she had a beautiful smile.

"Yogurt?"

Normally, the answer should have been no, because he happened to have balls, but what she called *yogurt* was basically a spoon of the stuff, put on top of a humongous meringue, and covered in fresh berries, so he nodded, watching her closely as she moved. Listening, too; she was right. She didn't make a noise; not when she stepped, anyway. The old cupboards betrayed her, but otherwise, the woman was incredibly quiet.

"You're a hunter."

It wasn't a question, and she nodded.

"I've been raised as one, yes. These days, I'm just a baker, though."

He sincerely doubted it.

Rygan sat on the high bar stool next to hers and grate-fully nodded when she gave him a plate of anything-but-yogurt. One mouthful, and he moaned, taking his untold words back. She *was* a baker, and a good one at that.

"What the fuck is in this?" he asked, because it couldn't be a damn meringue. At its center, there was a smooth mousse that tasted like heaven.

"That would be pistachio. I'm experimenting for a client who wants some for her wedding cake."

"Experiment successful."

All of a sudden, he understood why Daunte had asked if they could order from her bakery; he genuinely didn't think he'd eaten something that made him consider licking the plate in a long, long time. If there had been no witness, he totally would have, too.

"I don't know - I tried the mousse inside some choux yesterday - it worked a little better."

Fuck, he was hard. Thinking about *food*. Sweet food, too.

"Do you have any choux left?"

Aisling shook her head. "Nope. Ate two dozen of them, and my assistant finished the rest."

He scrutinized her, wondering where the fuck all the mousse, choux and other desserts she ate went. She had curves, but they were all in the right places; her wider hips, her generous ass. He was pretty sure no one able to inhale two dozen choux had the right to look like her. Their kind were generally slender, because of the exercise they all did in animal form, but still.

"So, Aisling. You know my last name, my height, my profession, and age. You also know what I look like in nothing but a towel. I just know you like to make grown men cry - be it by withholding choux or kicking their ass. Wanna even out the scale?"

"I don't know, I like being on top." His dick pushed against his zipper at the visual that conjured. "What do I get for telling you things about me?" she asked, her voice dipping low and suave, shooting right to his already hard cock, making it throb.

She was flirting, probably unaware that he was already fighting to prevent himself from laying her on the table and licking the sweet spot between her legs until she begged for mercy.

"What do you want?" he countered, his gaze intense.

She should have looked away; or rather, females would have. He was quickly learning not to expect her to behave like anyone else, though.

"You get a question, I get one. That's fair."
He nodded slowly, reluctantly. There were plenty of things he didn't like speaking about - namely, his

family and that was what most people were really curious about.

Aisling waved, inviting him to go first.

"Last name."

He'd looked around, and there were letters addressed to five different names on her mahogany dining room table.

Aisling shook her head. "Nope. I veto that one."

He immediately narrowed his eyes, wondering what reason she might have to hide it. Was she hiding from someone? Was she on the run?

"That's not how it works."

"It works how I say it works. Ask something else, or nothing at all. I don't care."

Rygan was too startled to speak at first; he couldn't remember anyone ever dismissing him that way before. It grated, but he accepted that the cards were in her hand, so he changed his question.

"Why are you a loner?"

He half expected her to blow him off again, but she answered. "I was part of a pride, once, and it didn't work out for me. It's supposed to be about supporting each other, but I'm a little different. So the flavor of the day was, *let's gang up on Aisling.* Not my thing."

Rygan nodded slowly, reluctantly - he knew it wasn't the whole truth.

"So, you weren't banished?"

"That's two questions," she said, rolling her eyes. "But I'll answer it - because you won't let this go unless I do. *No*, I wasn't banished. *No*, I'm no criminal. *Yes*, I've killed people - legally." That could mean a lot of things; in self-defense, or under contract approved by the government. One, he could understand, the other, he could respect. "And I will kill again," she added, "if I'm ever in a situation where I should. And *no*, you don't have the right to know everything I do. I'm not part of your pride, Alpha."

Taking the full strength of her gaze, Rygan wondered if that was what others felt when he glared at them. His tiger was pacing back and forth, uneasy at having that female pushing her dominance. She wasn't asking for his submission, though - she was simply answering with everything she had, to ensure he would know she was telling him the truth. No one could dominate without conviction.

He nodded. It wasn't like his hands were clean, anyway.

"My turn," she said, her amber gaze still intense. She tilted her head to the left a little again, and asked, "If I let you fuck me now, are you going to be clingy or move on and let me be?"

He didn't answer - he didn't need to. They both needed this. There was no other option; since the instant he saw her, he knew he was going to end up balls deep inside her.

There was nothing soft or refined about it - his teeth scraped her skin, she tore clothes from his limbs to free his cock, and took it in her greedy hands. They were animals, nothing more or less. Rygan took Aisling by the waist and popped her on the breakfast table, before placing himself between her legs, exactly where he'd wanted to be. His tiger was all for destroying her jeans and plunging his cock inside her, but he had other things on his mind. Sliding the denim down, along with her silken panties, he smirked and dived head first towards her pink, drenched folds.

"Oh fuck."

"Not yet."

She might have the upper hand in many things, but as she begged for mercy while his tongue lapped at her clit, wiggling in an attempt to break free, he was topping her in the only way that mattered.

Her breathing was coming in faster yet irregular, hitching, in places. She was close; so close. He could make her come now and then take her like he was desperate to. Get it over with. But at the back of his mind, something told him it would be just that: over. She was going to do what she'd said she would: move on, forget about him. The pretty kitty was careful - she liked the walls she'd constructed around her little world; he understood that. But nevertheless, he wanted to smash them down.

Rygan and his tiger were in perfect agreement right then. *Not now,* they both said. *We can wait.*

So, he came up for air, placing his throbbing cock at her entrance, and bending to reach her ear.

"What's your name?" he whispered, grinding against her clit.

He didn't expect her to answer; he expected her to bolt.

She did.

"Bastard."

"You need to come, pretty girl. And I'll give it to you - all I want in exchange is a name."

So, yeah, he was being an asshole. But a smart one. Aisling pushed his torso back and sat up, closing her legs.

"Right. Looks like I'll be finishing myself off, then," she huffed, turning away without another glance.

As he watched her sinful ass walk out, Rygan smiled like his balls weren't hating him right now.

He might not have fucked her, but he'd won the game

today. Aisling was a dominant female used to having what she wanted; she was going to be as obsessed with him as he was with her.

ANIMAL

*A*isling was cursing herself, wondering where her damn spine had run off to.

"Fucking Alpha," she grumbled under her breath while frosting a dozen cupcakes.

"Someone pissed you off?" Clarissa asked, entering the shop while counting dollar bills.

The orders were paid online or over the phone, and Aisling transferred Clary's salary by direct deposit, but her employee received plenty of tips with each delivery.

"Multiple someones," she replied, although it was perhaps a white lie.

While having a pride around pushed her buttons, it was Rygan and his damn tongue that she wanted to eviscerate for denying her a damn orgasm.

Okay, so she had been totally dumb to ask for it in the first place, but the man was downright cruel. She'd tried to get off at least five times after leaving him in the kitchen, without success. Her usually satisfying vibrator felt utterly inadequate compared to the smooth, thick, long cock he'd teased her with.

She bared her teeth, and squeezed her icing bag so hard the cupcake was drowned three inches of blueberry frosting.

"I'll have this one, thank you," Clary said, snatching the cake, and licking it with obvious glee. "So," she asked in between mouthfuls, "has your mood got anything to do with the bunch of hunks we've seen in town? People say they're shifters."

She grunted in response, but Clary wouldn't let it go.

"Do you know them?"

"I know one of them," she replied.

Aisling wasn't used to sharing; but somehow, one second she was looking in the baby blue eyes of her pretty assistant, and the next, she was spilling her guts. "This stays between us?"

Clary beamed at her, and like they were twelve, rather than twenty-four and twenty-eight, she extended her hand and curved her little finger.

"Pinky swear."

Ace stared at the finger like it might bite her.

"I do not pinky swear."

"You will if you want me to keep my mouth shut."

She could have just pointed out that she was happy to keep her affairs to herself, but Ace just shook her head, before briefly entangling her finger with Clary's, taking it back as quickly as she could.

"This never happened," she grumbled. Her reputation would take a hit if it ever got out. "Anyway, the Beta is my baby brother. The pride is getting targeted by wolves and he figured they could lie low here for a while."

Although she'd been put out when he'd first turned up, Aisling wasn't exactly pissed at Daunte, or surprised for that matter. She and her cat felt that it was perfectly natural that, in a time of danger, he'd turned to her. She wouldn't want it otherwise anyway.

"I didn't know you had a brother."

Ace shrugged. She never talked about Daunte - or the rest of her family.

It wasn't like she had any reason to want to hide them, directly - the issue was that everyone knew about Daunte's older sibling.

Tales about her were still a popular after dinner conversation in most prides. She felt no shame about any of the facts they knew about her; but being the subject of so much talk just pissed her off.

Still, Aisling was annoyed, and not only for the reasons she'd given her brother when he'd cornered her a couple of days back. Daunte had come with a complication that was unexpected and unappreciated. A delectable six foot four complication that made her cat bat her lashes like the slutty pussy she was.

She growled, and the currently cranky animal inside her snapped at her.

She didn't think they'd ever disagreed as much as they did now. Aisling wanted Daunte's pride out of her house as soon as possible. Her cat wanted to crawl to her brother's Alpha and jump on his cock. Repetitively.

She wanted kitties - always had - but normally, she agreed with Aisling that no male was worth their time. That Alpha...

THE SLUTTY CAT LIKED RYE, and it all came down to dominance.

Dominance was partially a genetic thing, and partially some Freudian shit that wasn't quite understood. No one was born dominant, just like no human was born overweight; some had a faster or a slower metabolism but ultimately, it came down to the individual's choices. Sometime around puberty, their dominance level was set for good and they learned to use it.

Submissives could use their vibes to diffuse situations -

the most powerful ones - the Omegas - were able to stop pissed off dominants in the middle of a conflict, calming them down. The strongest dominants had the ability to force obedience. All in all, both extremes could be dangerous.

Aisling had met exactly two feline shifters whose level of dominance equaled hers - her father, and her little brother. They'd never quite established who amongst them was the most dominant, and no one needed that question answered.

She felt comfortable enough in her family's company, knowing that she couldn't bend their will without meaning to; other shifters, she tiptoed around, unwilling to become a domineering ass. That was one of the many reason why she was unmated; she'd never tie herself to a male she could mold and she could mold everyone she'd ever met. She'd feel like shit about controlling someone else's actions - and besides, her cat wouldn't let her get involved.

Her brother's Alpha was another matter. He was as dominant as her - at least. She didn't know whether he was stronger; it wasn't impossible. She'd been pissed when Daunte had turned up at her doorstep with strangers; she could feel her cat infusing her every movement and there was no doubt that she'd also had her vibes working overtime. When she'd turned towards the intruders, all of them had taken a step back.

All of them, except him. He'd looked at her with no

fear, and his cat hadn't seemed startled either; she could feel him, barely under the surface.

Hers had clawed at her mind, demanding naughty things. But then, she'd seen the girl standing behind the Alpha, close to him, and snarled. The familiarity was enough to infuriate her cat.

DAMN STUPID PUSSY. Aisling had no interest in males; especially males who were part of a pride. She had a good life in Lakesides, with her bakery, her home, the amazing forest surrounding her - and when she felt an itch, she could find a human to scratch it somewhere in a nearby city. It wasn't like her to let some local male lick her out in her kitchen, even if he was only staying in the area temporarily.

But telling that to her cat right now was pointless. She wanted to be pinned under him again, and this time, she wouldn't let Aisling walk away.

Disagreeing with her cat felt weird; they normally felt the same way, as both of them liked simplicity. But the horny animal felt that jumping the Alpha was a pretty simple thing while Aisling knew it was anything but.

She had no business lusting after a guy like him. He was the Alpha of a pride that was staying around her territory; worse yet, he also was her *brother's* Alpha. That was too close to home and she preferred her flings to stay far, far away.

Basically the whole thing screamed *stay away*.

Her cat meowed in protest, focusing on what she found important - kitties. That hard cock that had been glistening against her could have given her kitties.

The animal didn't understand the subtleties of the nature of shifters. Even if Ace had wanted to - and she definitely didn't - she couldn't have just gotten herself pregnant by fucking another shifter. To procreate, they needed to be bound - by a blood oath, or a mating bond. She tried to explain it to her animal, who metaphorically stuck her little paws on her ears and chanted *can't hear ya, I want kitties*.

She sighed, and ignored the cat.

"Daunte is two or three years younger than me," Aisling replied to Clary.

"Two or three? You're not sure?"

This. This was why she didn't talk about her family.

"It's a long story."

She might have shared some of it, or might have left it alone; who knew? But she didn't, because just then, her ear vibrated, catching a faint change in the atmosphere around her.

There were wards around her town and her territory; she'd paid a witch friend of hers to place them, and maintain them. They'd been activated when Daunte and his pride had driven their bikes through it, warning her of their arrival.

And they were ringing again now.

ACE KNEW that one of the members of the pride had gone away a couple of days before - the short-haired enforcer. There was a good chance that she was just coming back.

Possibly. Maybe.

Still, she needed to check. Ace had plenty of enemies and it wouldn't do to let one of them walk in.

"Take care of the store," she told Clary, not taking the time to explain herself.

She walked out back, removing her clothes and shifted before leaving the bakery.

Finding the intruder took all of seven minutes; a sniff in his direction clarified that he was a wolf, which didn't say much. Someone she'd pissed off might have sent a wolf loner to scout the area and confirm her whereabouts. But as she found the man with a camera, taking pictures of the pride in her home, that spelled a different story.

It wasn't her problem. It *wasn't* her problem. She could just call Daunte and get him to track the wolf.

But then, just when she'd convinced herself to do that and go back to work, like she should, she saw the wolf's lens focusing on the kids playing in her backyard.

Her cat didn't wait for her authorization. She launched forwards, her claws digging deep inside the shifter's back.

The wolf screamed and attempted to shift, but before he could, she'd turned back to her human form. Changing forms took a lot of shifters close to a minute; being in perfect sync with her animal meant she could do it in the blink of an eye. He never saw that coming; before he knew it, she had him in a headlock.

The wolf struggled, cursing and even spitting at her, but no one had ever managed to make her let go, and it wasn't going to start now.

Shifters were considerably stronger than humans - even their weakest submissive, without any fighting skills, could defend themselves against a military trained officer - because of their animals. Like it or not, Aisling had an extra injection of feline gene, which made her twice the shifter in every way.

And sure, that meant that catnip had *embarrassing* effects on her, even when she was in human form, but it also meant that she had no problem grabbing the wolf under one arm, and carrying him, kicking and screaming, like he was just a toddler.

The commotion got some attention; a bunch of adult Wyvern cats were standing on her front porch, eyes focused on the two hundred pound of muscles she carelessly dragged along.

Rygan was frowning - a habit of his, from what she could tell - while Daunte smiled; Ola, Coveney, Tracy and Christine each bore an expression somewhere in between the Alpha's and the Beta's.

"What have we here?" Daunte asked, catching the wolf she tossed his way.

She shrugged.

"Your problem," she growled, annoyed that she'd intervened at all. "He was looking at you, not me."

So, yep. Maybe she was a little defensive.

She turned her heels, cursing herself for the second time that day, because half of her wanted to stay and see what the scout would reveal when the Wyvern played with him until he talked. But whoever said curiosity killed the cat might have had a point - she didn't want to find out. It *wasn't her problem.*

And anyway, she could always ask her brother later.

"Ace," Daunte chanted behind her. "If you don't stay now, I won't tell you what I've found out."

Dammit.

CONTACTS

*R*ygan's attention should have been entirely focused on the wolf strapped to a chair near the chimney, but it wasn't.

For the first time, he saw Aisling with his pride - or most of it. Ola and Christine had taken the children to their room; the rest of them stood in the lounge, snarling at the wolf.

Aisling should have stood out like a sore thumb, been an obvious outsider, made them feel uncomfortable. She didn't. The others weren't pushing her out with unwelcoming body language, except Kim, maybe, but she hardly counted. It seemed like she had a place amongst them.

His tiger agreed; he knew exactly what place he wanted her to have.

Rygan shouldn't have been surprised when he read the

animal's desires, but he was. He'd known she interested him; he hadn't realized that the tiger saw her as a potential partner. She was strong, and protective too - otherwise, she wouldn't have hunted that wolf for them. The animal saw her as an equal - a perfect Alpha.

Rygan narrowed his eyes. He saw everything his tiger pointed to, but he was the smart one here. He wouldn't let lust, and the fact that she was the first female the tiger liked, cloud his judgement. She was a loner, probably because she liked it that way. She'd said it herself; she hadn't been fond of living in a pride.

He'd fuck her - repetitively - while they lived in Lakesides. That much, he didn't doubt. They might even date; he had no objection to wining and dining her, if she was into that sort of thing. But thinking of her as a potential Alpha was premature, to say the least. For Christ's sake, he didn't even know her damn name.

"Aisling, do you have a chainsaw?" Ian asked, coming back from their SUV empty-handed. "I think we've left ours in the old house."

Their prisoner rolled his eyes.

"If you think that's going to intimidate me…"

Ian snorted.

"It's not to intimidate you. That's to go through your bones so we can bag you up when we're done."

That made the wolf stop smirking, now he realized there was no good cop who'd try to sweeten him up. They were going to kill him; how quickly depended on him.

"Look, we've all got things to do, so we'll keep things simple. I'm quite happy to snap your neck and get it over with, after you've told us what we need to know," Daunte said. "Or, we can remove your nails first, then cut your knuckles, dunk you, bleed you slowly - you get the picture. Tracy loves experimenting."

The young brunette smiled sweetly. "I write suspense books," she said with a wink. "*Please* say you don't want to talk. I can always use some new material."

The wolf got the picture; his eyes started to look around, hoping for something he could use, searching for a way out. With so many of them around him, he didn't have a chance, and he soon realized it, because he tried to negotiate.

"Hey, I was just under a simple contract. Someone hired me to find the Wyvern pride and bring back proof, that's all. If you let me go, I can tell them I've found you on the other coast."

Ian chuckled humorlessly.

"Or you could go back and sing like a canary. Sorry, man. Not taking that chance. Nothing personal."

He sounded matter of fact, almost bored. Rygan often left the interrogations up to him because his clinical detachment, paired with his cool demeanor, were pointblank frightening.

"You said you were hired. You're a loner."

That came from Aisling, who spoke softly, sounding soothing and sympathetic. Looked like they had a good cop after all.

"Yeah…wait, I know you."

"You might," she conceded.

Suddenly, the guy seemed fascinating to Rye.

"Where was the listing posted?" Ace asked, before he could do anything foolish - like change the direction of the interrogation.

The question didn't make sense to Rygan, but their prisoner replied, "The Lodge in L.A. Some suit came in, offering shit loads of money just for a tracking job."

Aisling fetched her phone and brought it to her ear; while it rang, she turned to Daunte and told him, "That guy knows nothing, just kill him."

The person she'd tried to reach on the line must have answered, because she started to speak.

"Hey, it's me. There's been a tracking contract recently. Yeah, that's right. Cancel it." A few second later, she thanked her contact. "You're the best."

Everyone was looking at her, except Daunte, who was bagging up the corpse of the wolf he'd just killed.

"How did you…"

"Not important." They all highly doubted that; but admittedly, it wasn't the most pressing matter right this second. "If your enemy went to the Lodge, they can pay a pretty penny, and they won't give up once they hear their contract was cancelled - I've just bought you time. You need to sort your shit before my town is turned in a fucking battlefield."

The woman was glowering, understandably pissed, but Rye was relieved to see that the anger didn't seem to be directed towards them.

"Look Ace, we've tried to negotiate, we've tried to contact the wolves we are allied to, and we've tried to track them. But we're a young pride," Daunte said. "We're not going to get far; not by ourselves."

Admitting it sucked, but the Beta had said it like it was. They just didn't have the right contacts; Rygan knew people of importance, but they weren't associated criminals, bounty hunters, and vengeful wolves. The most useful resource they had was Coveney, but the man couldn't hack information if they didn't know where to start.

The loner glared at Daunte until he said one simple word.

"Please?"

Her shoulders sagged. She flipped him off, and her phone was back on her ear.

"Hey Knox. Listen, I need you do to me a favor. Name your price. I'm not the one paying."

ONE HOUR. One hour - and a hundred thousand - was all it took, and they had answered. Names, details.

"I don't even know the Vergas pack," Daunte said, shaking his head.

"They're pretty big in wolf circles," Ian interjected.

Rygan nodded; he remembered hearing quite a few things about them.

"They're purists; even their own kind finds them excessive. They don't accept matings between wolves and other kinds of shifters, or humans. Wolves that can't shift by puberty get killed, and the parents don't have the right to give birth to other children after that. But they pretty much stick to wolf affairs."

It didn't make a blink of sense; why would they be after them?

He must have said it out loud, because Ace replied, "Their issue is your toddler."

Those who didn't growl protectively hissed; well, Kim didn't, but no one cared.

"The youngest. She has wolf in her, right?"

They exchanged glances.

Honestly, Lola had always been hard to place, her scent and behavior didn't quite fit any feline they could think of - not unlike Aisling, really - but Rygan had never wondered if she was a hybrid, because they were *rare*. Very, very rare.

The only way shifters could have children was if they were bound by blood, or mated. The blood ceremony that couples went through after getting married worked between shifters of the same species, or between a shifter and a human; no one knew why, but it didn't completely bind shifters of different species - feline and wolves, or birds and bears. They sometimes married, but they never reproduced.

However, fated mates were a completely different matter.

MATED PAIRS WERE RARE, although a little more common over the last century as they had been in the past - being able to travel the globe helped. But what he knew of the dozen of mated shifters he'd met was that they'd all become infinitely stronger. There was a pair of mated Omegas who'd singlehandedly stopped the shifter wars down in Mexico. In Canada, two mated Alphas ruled the entire country; they were wolves, but every race, feline included, obeyed their commands. Of course, not every mated pair took political functions, but they had one thing in common: power.

Rygan knew that a cross-species mating could result in children, but there hadn't been one for centuries, to his knowledge.

"Okay, so let's talk hypothetically," Tracy reasoned. "Let's say I was a wolf, part of the Vergas Pack, and I mated a feline. I'd know that I, along with my mate and child, would be hunted down."

"So, I'd give my toddler to someone who isn't likely to give it up to a pack of wolves - a pride of felines."

Suddenly, it all made sense.

"Right, well, we can give them Lola and they'll be off our case then."

They all turned to Kim, who rolled her eyes and said, "Joke. Duh."

Only, Rye wasn't certain she had been joking. The woman was that shallow.

"They won't get their hands on her," Rygan stated. "Not while any of us are still breathing."

He was purposefully looking at Ace when he said that, as if daring her to contradict him, telling them she was leaving them to their own mess. He half expected her to; but instead, the woman nodded, sealing her fate.

Alright, Rye reluctantly told his tiger. The beast might

have had a point. He had to agree that she might somewhat make a suitable Alpha female after all.

That was, if he ever convince her to give him a chance. Oh, and also, join his pride, when she obviously loved her freedom.

Good thing he'd never been one to run from a challenge.

WILD

*F*ucking hell. What had she gotten herself into? All because the damn sexy Alpha had hypnotized her with all his manliness.

Aisling shook her head; if she was honest, she was lying to herself. She'd pledged to help because the barbarians needed killing. Badly. Going after an innocent child wasn't flying with her - not at all.

But they were going against a gigantic, well-connected pack of wolves. That wasn't going to be pretty.

Fuck.

Needing a reprieve from her own home - even upstairs, she could smell the spicy, musky scent of the male who drove her mad - she ran out the window, landing on a nearby branch, and ran along the trees until she was deep within the forest.

Then, after leaving her clothes on a neat pile, she shifted...and the fucking cat immediately turned around, heading back towards the house.

Aisling had to laugh. The animal was impossible.

She could have shifted back, but there was no need to - caging her animal was never a good idea, and contrary to just about any other shifter out there, Aisling could actually hang around others without alarming them.

Her soft paws expertly made it back inside the house and she went to perch on her favorite tree, where she liked to observe the newcomers.

Coveney, the tall, dark and handsome Head Enforcer, was fluent in grunts, but she didn't think she'd heard him say much. Daunte, as per usual, was the life of the party, smiling when he didn't laugh. Ian spent most of his time behind his laptop, but never seemed to miss a word of the conversation going on around him. Christine - the woman who'd ridden on Rygan's bike - was sassy and outspoken, although she was clearly submissive, while Tracy, a dominant, read quietly in a corner. Ola seemed to be the caretaker, focusing on the children; Aisling recognized Hsu as the Seer, because she occasionally spoke of the future as though it was set in stone. "Don't worry when you pick Niamh up late, tomorrow. She'll make new friends at the grocery store."

Niamh was the only one of their children who wasn't

a werecat; in fact, she wasn't a shifter at all. If Aisling wasn't mistaken, the kid was actually a witch. She knew plenty of witches with auras similar to hers, in any case. Then, there was Lola, the youngest, who was often glued to Rygan; the reason behind all their trouble was an adorable little thing who still sucked on her thumb.

Jasper, Clive, Victoria, Daniel and Will were around the same age, and acting like siblings, although none of them had any features in common.

Her cat purred, soaking in the atmosphere, and Aisling felt a pang of regret. The loner life was better for her, but there was no denying that her cat missed the sense of belonging a pride could bring.

Although frankly? She'd never known it. Aisling might have lived in a pride for a dozen years or so, but she had never been *part* of one.

AISLING AND DAUNTE'S father wasn't all there. Actually, scratch that. He was a pointblank lunatic and his nickname, The Butcher, was a euphemism. Nowadays, he was just a little unstable around the edges, but thirty years ago? That had been another story altogether.

Aisling knew other shifters felt sick to their stomach every time they heard the story but to her, it was just a fact. Just her life.

Her father had been feral - completely wild, never shifting back to his human form. As such, he mated with an actual animal. There was nothing wrong about it, as far as she was concerned because, well, he *had* been an animal, too.

She would have preferred if he'd picked a panther, a lynx, a margay - just about anything, really - but somehow, The Butcher mated with a Savannah; a breed that was a mix between a serval and a domestic cat. They were pretty and delicate, so she supposed it meant the man had good taste.

Either way, like it or not, those were her parents. A shifter and a cat.

She wasn't sure how long she'd lived in the wild, two, three years maybe. But she hadn't known better; she was smarter than her mother, and she questioned more - but as far as she had known, Aisling had been a cat.

Eventually, the pretty Savannah died. Aisling mourned her without being able to express it, not understanding the feeling that wasn't quite natural in the forest. Death was part of life and another cat - an adult cat - would have moved on. She didn't. She cried and stayed with the carcass for days. She still remembered the smell of the rotting corpse, and the way she'd had to fight against the predator who'd wanted to eat it.

But then he'd arrived. The smooth, big biped. She recognized his scent; she smelled exactly like the leopard who looked at her and her mother from afar some times, never attacking them. *Safe*, she thought. So, she let him approach, only scratching when he moved to touch the broken corpse.

The man ignored her hisses and warning claws, held her up by the scruff of her neck, and popped her on his shoulder.

"Stay here."

It sounded like a weird growl to her, but while she didn't understand the words, she obeyed his dominant order.

He buried her mother deep, so that no other animal would harm her. The grave was unmarked, but she could still exactly pinpoint the place where it had happened.

Then, her father took her home.

It took two years for her to shift to human form, and she didn't talk before she was ten. However, she could hunt, and kill just about anything, completely at peace with her animal.

Aisling was a legend - everyone knew of The Butcher's first child. Especially since she'd taken on some jobs as a bounty hunter after leaving her pride the minute she'd turned eighteen.

The pride members had been frightened of her - understandably - and that meant that the kids had bullied her, while the adults treated her like trash and blamed her for everything that ever happened.

Her pride did one thing right. She'd left ten years ago, and still, no one knew she was a girl; The Butcher's first child, as far as the world knew, was a gruff, illiterate, grunting hunter who never shifted to his human form - not a bookish baker. The Alpha might have given them all an order to keep it secret, frightened of what would happen to them if she was thrown under the bus.

Oh, she wouldn't bother them - as far as she was concerned, they were nothing more than a bad memory. But her father, who still lived with them in Maryland, might have seen things differently. The Alpha wasn't stupid. He knew The Butcher could and would kill him, if he ever felt like it.

SHE WAS SNAPPED BACK from memory lane and her cat lifted her pretty head when someone cooed at her, flattered by the words and soothed by the tone. *Of course* it had to be the damn Alpha she wanted to jump.

Rygan.

Rygan Wayland. She'd googled him the minute she'd been alone after her brother had given her his name.

Second son of the Ruler of all feline shifters in the US,

Rygan had formed his own pack after his current Head Enforcer, Coveney, had wrongfully been accused of raping some important guy's daughter. He probably hadn't wanted the man to become a loner - a hated loner, at that. Coveney had been a close friend of his and, going against most of his pride and all his family, he supported him. He was followed by another one of his friends, Ian, Ola, an apprentice healer, and Christine, a submissive. Ace wasn't sure how or when the others had joined, but she knew Daunte had turned eighteen a couple of years after the whole drama; he immediately asked to be transferred to his pride.

About six years ago, the woman who'd started the whole mess had come forward to retract her accusation, but by then, the Wyvern Pride had been fully formed, and completely independent.

Rygan wasn't all heart and flowers. His linage and the size of his pride made him a prime target for any idiot wanting to make a name for himself by killing a werecat prince, so he'd been attacked numerous times, and each time, he and his small pride had left dozens of corpses - wolves, hyenas, crows - anything that had come at them. The Vergas pack was a different kind of enemy, though - they were large, resourceful, and determined. Worse yet: they genuinely believed they were doing the right thing, and that made them dangerous.

Still, Ace thought the pride had a good chance of

making it. Honestly, when she'd first learned about the small pride Daunte had joined, she'd assumed that they survived attacks thanks to her brother, but now, she wasn't so sure. Rye looked like he'd enjoy a blood-bath almost as much as the next psycho.

He was broad, tall, lean but muscular, and his dark grey eyes could be cold, when he wasn't cooing and calling her "pretty kitty."

And what did her damn slutty pussy do? She jumped down, and rubbed against his leg.

Rygan scratched her fur, making her purr like her life depended on it; then he actually scooped her up in his arms.

Now was the time to be a badass and scratch the heck out of him. *Any minute.* Aisling scowled at her cat, who stretched in his arms, baring her belly as if to say *"Scratch me theeeeere."*

And the damn Alpha did.

She was infuriated. But as she was also getting a tummy rub, she was infuriated while daydreaming of freaking rainbows and pink unicorns.

"Rye, are you going to take over from Coveney? He hasn't eaten yet."

The Alpha sighed, and gently popped her down on the floor, telling her, "See you later, kitty cat. It appears I have some work to do," with one last scratch between her ears.

He walked out of the house, which didn't please her cat - the damn hussy pussy just followed him, softly, silently.

She found his clothes on the back door's steps and felt a jolt of excitement at the prospect of meeting his cat.

Oh, no, no, no. No way, no how.

Rygan wasn't an idiot, or a weirdo like her father, but there was no doubt in her mind that her damn cat was going to do her best to get mounted, which would be so fucking embarrassing she might die on the spot, so she started to force the shift, but before her cat had relented, she found herself face to face with a goddamn sabertooth tiger.

She was pretty certain those things were supposed to be extinct. Was he wearing some kind of fake kitty fangs?

Aisling tilted her head, intrigued and cautious, but her cat didn't give a damn. She wanted to *plaaaaaay*. The animal, who was comparatively tiny, had decided that the humongous beast in front of her was an appropriate playmate. Idiot.

However, as she was relatively confident her cat currently was more interested in playing hide and seek than getting fucked, she let her do her routine, trot around and rub against the banisters.

You're not afraid.

Her cat wasn't, but Aisling, however, was freaked out. Big time.

They weren't part of the same pride and they'd never exchanged blood, so she was *not* supposed to hear Rygan in her damn head. But she let it slide, preventing herself from responding. If she did, he'd know she was a shifter.

Aisling had one advantage over others of her kind: there was more animal than human in her, which meant that when she did shift in her animal form, her human scent was almost negligible. Shifters who didn't know better never realized she was one of them, in that form. That had been a tremendous help, back when she'd been a bounty hunter.

The tiger in front of her lowered his head, back side lifted, and pounced on her - delighted, her stupid cat ran around, and Aisling must have been totally stupid, too, because she was smiling like a crazy person. Having fun. It had been a while she'd played with a cat - Daunte visited, but they rarely shifted.

Regretfully, Rygan's tiger stopped after a while and slowly walked towards the border of her territory, where they met another tiger - a normal one this time. No weird fangs.

Aisling didn't hear their mental conversation, which was a relief; although it didn't explain how she heard

Rygan in the first place. They conversed while her cat stayed close by, cleaning her claws. Coveney - she recognized his scent - asked about her, she could feel it. He seemed open to play, too, because that was what cats did, when they didn't fuck, or sleep - but her cat just looked at him with utter contempt.

The cat was such an ass. Aisling was silently laughing and shaking her head. But what could she say? The girl had standards.

DECISIONS

*R*ygan woke up alone, although he'd fallen asleep on the grass next to the female who had tired him out.

That sounded like the best kind of naughty in the world, but as he was talking about an actual cat - of the non-shifting variety - he'd just run trying to catch her until he couldn't move another muscle. Damn kitty was quick.

"Waking up just in time for a Cuban," Daunte said, holding a box of cigars up. "Want one?"

Rygan stretched languorously, before shifting.

He was pretty sure the reason why he got along with his Beta so well was because they were both freaks of sort - or in any case, Daunte had been raised by one. He understood.

Rygan might not be completely mad like The Butcher, but he had the same effect on people - they feared him, because he was bigger than any feline shifter out there. Those deadly white fangs coming out from under his upper lip probably didn't help.

His pack members were used to it, but at first, they all shuddered. In fact, he'd never met anyone who didn't. Except Daunte. And that pretty Savannah-ish cat, too.

He found himself wondering, "What is he like? Your older brother." The one person who was seen as more freakish than him by their community. "You never speak of him."

Daunte was pretty open to sharing information about his father, the way he'd raised him; he'd even put the enforcers through some of the training The Butcher had taught him, but Rygan couldn't recall one time when he'd mentioned his notorious sibling.

Rygan understood. He wasn't particularly fond of speaking about his own brother, Colter, his father's heir, so he'd never asked.

Colter was perfect - strong, smart, reliable. Whatever Rygan accomplished, Colter had already done it, and that completely negated his value, as far as his old pride had been concerned. He'd been expected to excel, because his brother had before him. The first time Rye had become his own person, rather than a King's lesser son and a Prince's brother, was when he'd created his pack. Even then, no one had supported his decision.

As he'd had more than two members following him, no one could legally deny his application to form the Wyvern pride, but they had all been as unsupportive as possible; except Rygan's grandmother.

The old crone was yet another Colter groupie, and she had never been very fond of Rye, yet she was the one who'd made it down to the hotel where they'd stayed while deciding on a direction, a large check in hand. He still didn't understand it, but one day, he was going to have to thank her for it. As that meant going to his father's territory, or attending the Fest, it wasn't very high in his list of priorities.

"Ah, yes. My sibling. Half of what you've heard is probably true, the other half couldn't be more inaccurate."

Rygan waggled an eyebrow, wondering when his Beta had taken to talking in riddles.

"We get along. There's no doubt that we have each other's back. But yep. He's a crazy motherfucker and he'll tear through someone's skull in a heartbeat - for the right reasons."

Rygan smiled, smoking his cigar.

"That makes two of us."

He'd cracked a skull or two in his time.

"If we get the house, we'll need to purchase it under the umbrella of one of Ian's companies, or a fake name. The wolves will find us eventually, but let's not make it easy on them."

He didn't always understand the details of Hsu's visions, as the images flew too quickly, but there was no doubt that a battle was still coming; when she'd seen what happened here, though, the results of the battle was everyone coming home; battered, exhausted, but alive. The kids, Ola and Christine were also fine. Something had made a difference in Lakesides; perhaps there was a hide-out the wolves wouldn't find.

Doubtful. Wolves were the best trackers; their damn noses were naturally better than any feline's. Rye was missing something.

"You look worried. I mean, more than usual."

Rygan sighed.

"I think Hsu's vision might make us complacent. Now we know what's after us, I don't see any reason why the pride should be safer here than anywhere else, so we need to be vigilant."

Daunte looked like he might want to say something but after a second, he just nodded.

"I'll patrol, if you want to go back to bed. You've barely slept for days. You need a few hours in a row, Alpha - not twenty minutes here and there."

Rye nodded, thankful, and headed inside.

Daunte was right, he wouldn't be any good to the pride completely sleep deprived, so he went to the small bedroom, and dropped on the twin bed. He was asleep before his head hit the pillow.

RYE WAS AWOKEN by one of the most pleasing sensations in the world, a soft hand running along his cock, a wet tongue lapping at it, but something was wrong; he knew it before opening his eyes. Instead of feeling aroused, he was revolted, and also pretty confused.

"What the fuck are you doing?" he yelled, pushing Kim's hand away.

It didn't make a bit of sense.

Okay, so maybe he'd been stupid, years ago, when she first joined his pack; he might have screwed the woman once or twice, but he'd made it absolutely clear that he was done a long time ago, and she had seemed okay with it. She'd just gone to the rest of the males in the pride to satisfy her needs - Daunte, Ian, and Coveney had all obliged; sometimes, together, from what he'd heard. The woman had three holes and knew how to use them.

Rye hated the term, but for lack of better words, she really was the pride whore. She had no other use.

What she'd done now wasn't going to fly. He wouldn't

have minded if she'd just made the move on him; he would simply have rejected her, and that would've been that, but touching him while he slept, without his consent? That wasn't acceptable. They didn't have that sort of relationship and she damn well knew it.

"I see you looking at me," she purred, batting her long lashes. "I came to give us what we both want."

Right. So the girl was delusional.

"What was that?"

He was just dumbfounded. If he ever looked at her, it was with contempt.

Ten years ago, he'd been young, restless, as well as overwhelmed with all the duties suddenly entrusted to him, so he'd welcomed the distraction. Pounding the hole between her long legs had given him an outlet for a few minutes here and there, but he'd since realized just how pitiful and self-centered Kim was, and she had completely lost her appeal. Plus, he didn't judge the others for doing it, but he'd never fuck a woman who'd gone through all his pridemates.

"I don't know what you been smoking, but I don't want you. Never have, actually; you were just there."

Cruel, but she'd gone too far when she'd come to his room and put her fucking hands on him without permission. It was past time to make it clear what her place was. By that, he meant that she had none. She hadn't taken any duty in the pride, she didn't even cook or clean; she just hung with them, using their resources like a damn parasite. He put up with it because Jas, her twin, did far more than her share, but enough was enough. He wasn't going to let Kim get away with that sort of shit.

A lot of prides, and packs, kept official sluts onboard, both male and female - shifters weren't shy about sexuality, and it wasn't always easy to meet their needs outside of their territories. Having one or two members ready to fuck when they needed to made things simpler.

The notion was old fashioned and, as far as Rye was concerned, disgusting. Animals also licked shit off their peer's ass - it didn't mean that they had to do it.

He mostly ignored it. Kim was more than willing; she'd reduced herself to being their whore, voluntarily, and he knew his enforcers had never crossed the line - they never even went to her, she was the one doing the seducing.

She looked confused, which in other circumstances might have been fucking hilarious; he hadn't exactly minced his words. Anyone with self-respect would already have been out of the room, but there she stood, with a pot of make up on her face, too much perfume and her huge tits hanging out of her negligée.

She was surprised because shifters weren't prudes -

they loved sex, and her advances were probably welcomed whenever she bestowed them.

"It's about her, isn't it? The loner."

A growl formed in his throat.

"No, Kim. It's about you having screwed every single male of the pride. It's about you not pulling your weight, and it's about me not being into you."

And perhaps it was *a little* about Rye wanting Ace so much his somnolent appendage, repulsed by Kim's hands, twitched as he thought of her.

"I'm going to go take a shower. Get out of my room before I come back."

PLAYED

*N*ow they had a better idea of what was
going on, finding more details about their
enemies wasn't hard for Coveney.

He looked into the Vergas Pride, and came back with
a somber expression. He explained the basics.

Apparently, the pride was humongous, with over five
hundred adult members overall; it practically took
over a whole town down in Texas. No wonder they
had no issue fighting them on two fronts.

"So far, they haven't sent their full force, presumably
because they haven't confirmed Lola is the kid they're
after. They're targeting a few different prides and
packs with children fitting her description. For all we
know, it *could* be that she isn't the hybrid."

Rye wasn't so sure; after Ace had pointed out their

toddler had a faint lupine scent, he'd been able to notice it, too.

"Not all of them are fighters, though, right?" Christine asked, but Coveney shook his head, pushing another stack of printed pictures in her hand.

The submissive gasped and let the documents drop to her feet.

The details he printed made everyone sick to their stomach. What the fucking hell was that?

"Are those... skeletons?"

It was hard to tell, because they'd been burned to a crisp and stacked together, but Coveney nodded.

"They kill their own members; the ones they see as useless. As far as they're concerned, only the strongest have the right to live - the others are lesser beings. They don't want them to reproduce, so they take the problem out of the equation. So, only the fighters survive."

"They murder the submissives?" Ola sounded light-headed, faint.

"Not all of them. Those pretty enough are kept, and used as slaves, if anyone wants to claim them. They see it as the survival of the fittest."

How fucking barbaric. It didn't make a bit of sense, no animal in the world acted that way.

This pack of degenerated fanatics had to be stopped,

but how? They had considerably more members than them, and that was without considering the fact that they might have some allies who'd join them in an open conflict.

"If we talk at the Fest, we might find other prides who want to join us against them," Tracy suggested.

Rygan shook his head. It might have been an option, if the next summer gathering wasn't months away. They didn't have the luxury of time, not while those monsters were on their trail, hunting their youngest, most vulnerable child.

"We can't wait," he replied.

"How about contacting the Alphas we know online?" Dante proposed.

Rye nodded his agreement; that was a viable option. There was a fair chance that his father might even agree to help them, given the circumstances...but he didn't have the best relationship with his family, so he couldn't count on it.

And frankly, even if every single feline in his acquaintance agreed to lend them a hand, they would still be outnumbered.

"We need to show this to Ace," he decided, weirded out by the fact that he felt compelled to share the details with her.

"I can go talk to her," the Beta offered, but Rye was quick to reject that option.

"I don't think so. I'll go after the auction." His answer was cold, possessiveness dripping from each word, making him uncivil towards his Beta. "Speaking of, we need to head out now."

THE HOUSE they had their eyes on was getting auctioned off in Lakesides that day.

Rye felt the gaze of everyone on him, his Beta and his Enforcer as they walked into the town hall. They were all human which explained why he sensed so much fear and suspicion.

He could guess what the whispers said. They wouldn't let them win if they could help it; they didn't want them in town. He paid the humans no mind, taking a seat at the back. He'd buy the house - that's all there was to it. Feeling unwelcome wasn't a foreign concept anyway. It wasn't like there was a better alternative elsewhere - according to recent censuses, there were about two hundred humans for every supernatural creature out there. That meant there was no place where his pride would really be unanimously accepted.

Some people kept it civil, nodding towards them - he returned the greeting. Those who openly glared, he ignored.

All of a sudden, the atmosphere completely changed; it almost felt like everyone in the room sighed in relief.

As for Rye, he felt the corner of his mouth curve up. He hadn't expected Ace to come.

A middle-aged man, slightly rounded around the edges, and with greying hair, greeted her with enthusiasm.

"Aisling, dear. Are you here to bid on the house? It's a beauty. I had it done up by the best of the best."

The owner, then.

There was an eagerness to his words; he was clearly hoping that the group of newcomers he didn't trust would find some competition.

Ace smiled sweetly, dazzling the poor unsuspecting human, and playing him like a damn violin.

"I'm not," she confessed, "I'm just here to see if my friends get it. Come, let me introduce you."

She entwined her arm with the old man's and made him follow her to the back of the room, where the pride members had chosen to sit.

"Guys, this is Andrew Turner. He knows everything there is to know about Lakesides' history, if you have any questions."

The man lifted his chin proudly.

"Andrew is the mayor of this town, and the owner of the house you would like to buy." She looked up at him, her big amber eyes shining as she batted her long lashes. Fuck, the woman was lethal. "This is a few members of the Wyvren pride. They're a new pride of feline shifters - like me - and they've encountered some trouble. You see, they adopt orphans, and it turns out some people want to harm one of their children."

Rye wasn't exactly happy that she'd divulged their affairs so openly, but the mayor frowned.

"Children?" he repeated, turning to the pride.

Rygan nodded. "They're after a two year old."

The other humans, who were shamelessly eavesdropping, gathered around them; the glaring had stopped, replaced by curiosity and, if Rye wasn't mistaken, protectiveness. Holy fuck. *Humans* were being cool with shifters. What the hell was happening with the world?

"This is Rygan, the Alpha," Ace introduced, pointing to him. "And Daunte, the Beta. You've met him a couple of times in the past, right?"

"Aye," a guy in the crowd said, nodding. "You came to my pub last year. Pretty good at pool, aren't you?"

She played them so damn easily. In a minute, she'd established that the Beta - one of the highest authorities in the pride - had already come to their town without causing any trouble, and she'd also made it clear that they needed their help; something the small town people apparently responded to.

"Tracy is a bestselling author," she added; that seemed to impress - Rye guessed the town didn't see many celebrities. "They've stayed at my place this week, and they want to buy your house because of the security measures you've taken. The windows are reinforced, aren't they?"

"Yes; it was originally made for my daughter, when she was single," Andrew explained. "Only the best for my girl. The fences are electrified, too."

When the auction started, the humans sat around them; they all glared at the couple of investors wearing suits. The pride won - they weren't going to let this opportunity pass, even if they'd had to overpay for the house - and everyone clapped.

"You can move in today, it's empty," the mayor told them. "We'll take care of the paperwork by the end of the week."

Others said a variation of, "You got a problem, you call. No one should target kids."

Rye just stared at Ace, dumbfounded. She winked before getting up.

"Right. I'd better get back to work - poor Clary has been alone for over an hour."

TEASE

*R*ygan was annoyed, and more annoyed yet, because quite frankly, he had zero reason to be pissed at all. They'd won the house they wanted, buying it for a pittance; if they left, they could flip it and make a decent profit. His keen sense of business should have put him in a good mood, but instead, he wanted someone to punch.

If. He'd thought *if* they left the house - when it was a question of *when*. They were going to leave. Thinking otherwise was just going to set him up for disappointment.

The problem wasn't as much leaving Lakesides - although he'd taken to the quiet town and its weird inhabitants - as it was knowing that he'd leave a certain loner behind...

"What's the matter?" Tracy asked, frowning.

He noticed that he was growling low, threateningly.

Dammit. He and his tiger had never been as unsettled as they had been since their arrival in Lakeside. The animal had wanted him to follow Ace around like a damn lost puppy, and had started to sulk when Rygan wouldn't give in.

It was as though…

No. He wasn't going to start thinking nonsense now. He was attracted to and intrigued by Aisling, no doubt about that, but attraction happened every day. Having a hard on for a woman didn't mean that she was his mate, his other half, shaped by nature to complete him.

MATINGS HAD BEEN STUDIED over the three decades since the paranormal community had revealed themselves to the rest of the world. Shifters, angels, demons, vampires, and everything in between had fated mates, and no scientist had come up with definite information; they just had theories, at best. Some said mates were the results of an evolutionary thing: nature picked two people who were likely to have strong children, and bound them together. That theory was destroyed by the fact that sometimes, true mates were of the same sex, and therefore unable to reproduce.

Rye didn't care about the logic behind it. All he knew was that, as a shifter, he had two choices - getting married and blood-bound to someone he cared about, some day, or waiting in the hopes of meeting that one person designed for him, and share everything, heart, soul, and blood.

He was already stronger than he cared to acknowledge, and patience had never been his forte. Besides, he was thirty-one. Like many before him, he was more than happy to go with option one: find someone to spend his life with. Find someone who wouldn't be in his head constantly - someone who couldn't control him. He might already have settled down if his damn tiger had been more compliant. But no, out of all the women he'd met, the stupid animal had to pick *that one*. The one who came with a warning label.

Still. That didn't mean that the woman was his mate.

It *didn't*. Most other feline shifters he knew were attracted to women left, right, and center. Their animals sometimes agreed with them, letting them form relationships, temporary or otherwise. Ace might have been the first that the grumpy tiger found fetching but it meant nothing.

Nothing at all.

His head snapped left as his nostrils took in a scent that shouldn't already be so familiar. Wood, earth, spices, currently mixed with butter and honeycomb. There she was, behind the window of a pretty, elegant bakery, giving a frosted cupcake to a little girl. Then, she leaned over the counter and handed one to the human guy accompanying the child, along with her most open, dazzling smile.

He didn't like that at all.

"Rye?"

"Go ahead," he told Daunte. "Start packing. I've got to speak to her about the Vergas wolves."

The Beta nodded and walked away; when Rye turned back, the customer and his daughter had also left the bakery, and Aisling was cleaning the counter. A tall, pretty woman in her twenties appeared from the back, and Ace gave her a few boxes, as well as a cupcake - a yellow one, this time.

He was staring like an idiotic creeper and he didn't like it, so he shook his head, and walked in.

The instant he pushed the door open, the woman snarled and when she lifted her eyes to his, they were golden. Dangerous. Sexy as fuck. Take your pick.

"What are you doing here? I thought we'd agreed to stay away from each other."

He could have pointed out that she'd been the first to ignore her own rule when she'd turned up at the auction, but he just replied, "The angry look doesn't work on me, kitty cat. It just turns me on."

She dropped the snarl and sighed, muttering, "Weirdo."

He couldn't deny that.

"So, you're really into sweet things, aren't you?"

While she had some savory rolls and breads on one side, the star of the show was her impressive display of cupcakes, mini pies and muffins.

She crossed her arms and mumbled defensively, "It sells. What are you doing here?"

"The smell led me here," he said truthfully.

Only it was her scent rather than cupcakes that had forced his steps.

"Well, what can I tempt you with?"

He waggled an eyebrow, because if he wasn't mistaken, that qualified as flirting.

"What's on the menu?" Rygan shot back, his eyes fixed on hers.

The woman was going to be the death of him; he knew it for a fact when she took another cupcake and plunged her finger in the frosting. She lifted her finger to his mouth, saying, "Open."

Rygan obeyed. He didn't have any other choice.

Then, she brought the same finger to her own mouth and licked it clean, before sucking it for good measure.

Fucking. Hell.

"What do you say; a little too spicy for you?"

He was *this close* to jumping on the other side of the

counter and throw her on his shoulder, but something told him that little show wasn't seduction as much as a display of dominance. Glaring hadn't worked, so she showed she was on top by manipulating him, instead.

"You don't want to play that game with me, pretty girl," he warned her, edging over the counter. "It'll end with your ass reddened by my palm."

"Aww," she shot back, with a condescending and adorable moue. "I didn't know you were delusional. There's a really good shrink in town, if you want the contact details."

A bell rang and the door of her bakery opened; he didn't have to turn to hear the three sets of heavy human footstep, or smell the overly flowery perfumes. Aisling's gaze lost its amusement, and she regained a professional demeanor.

Rygan got the message; he wasn't going to mess things up for her at work. Reluctantly, he took a step back.

"I'll take a dozen cupcakes."

"Which flavors?" she asked, shooting him a fucking infuriating forced, professional smile.

"Two of each."

"Coming right up."

She carefully placed the cakes in a beige box and wrapped it with a blue ribbon, before handing it to him.

"How much do I owe you?"

"It's on Daunte's tab," she replied with a shrug.

Somehow that annoyed him.

"Not necessary. I can pay myself."

She glared but replied, "eighteen dollars."

"They're two dollars each."

She was giving him a discount? Did anything make sense about that woman?

"Twenty-four dollars then!"

She didn't stamp her foot, but she visibly wanted to. Rygan smiled, ridiculously glad to be able to get under her skin.

He popped some money at the counter, leaving his card on top of it.

"Call me when you're done here. I actually came on business."

"DAMMIT, Ian, watch where you're going," Rye growled at the poor schmuck who was carrying a box so large he couldn't physically see a thing.

Rygan knew he was being a dick, but he couldn't help it. He was in a foul mood, no point denying it. Preparing to leave Aisling's home felt...wrong. His tiger was roaring in protest, not letting him catch a break.

"You know, I'd say your tiger can make the run between her house and ours in fifteen minutes, max. Chin up."

Rye turned to his Beta, eyes narrowed. From the very start, he'd seen the man as a rival of sorts, because it was clear that he and Aisling were friendly, but Daunte wasn't jealous at all; if anything the man just seemed amused by the situation, smirking whenever he caught the heated looks Rye and Ace exchanged.

"Chill. I really don't want into her pants. We're *literally* like family. I'd give you the whole *don't hurt her* speech, but honestly, I'm more worried about her cutting your balls off and feeding them to you if you ever do something you shouldn't."

Rye winced, admitting that she probably would.

"So you just see her like a little sister, then?"

Daunte shook his head.

"Nope. I'm the baby here. You know Ace's twenty-eight, right?"

That would be a no. Actually, hell to the no. She looked twenty-one, tops.

"It's the dimples. They make her look adorable."

"And she'd cut *your* balls off for calling her that."

"Which is why I'm not saying it to her face."

Rye laughed; he was glad to have been mistaken when he'd believed that his Beta was involved with his…

His what?

Suddenly, he realized something. If Ace wasn't Daunte's conquest…

"She's from your old pride," Rye guessed, and Daunte immediately closed up.

Rygan smirked; it had only lasted an instant but the startled look the Beta had sent her made him think he'd nailed that one.

"Come on, Daunte. I don't mean her any harm."

The beta nodded. "Sure. But it's her history - *she's* the one who wants to keep it private. How do you think she'll feel if you sniff around until you get your answers? Let me give you one clue about Ace - she's wounded. She has a chip on her shoulder, and she never got over it. And how do you get a wounded animal's trust?"

He didn't answer the rhetorical question. They both knew: you let it come to you.

Rye nodded slowly.

"By the way, there may or may not be a few bets going about you two. I have five hundred bucks in the pot, so don't mess up."

DISCOVERY

Okay, so maybe he'd hated leaving Ace's place, but now that they'd made it to their new home, he wasn't exactly complaining. The place rocked. There was more space than they were used to, the latest technology, under flooring heating, and the security was completely over the top, which meant that he saw it as adequate. It was perfect; or it would be, when he could drag Ace's ass there.

"You want to see the master bedroom," Daunte told him, pointing up the stairs.

Rye shifted, letting his animal have his fun; he wanted to know if he could easily navigate through their new home. The wide staircases weren't a problem. He got to the first floor and quickly investigated the space, nodding at the nine sun-filled, large and elegant rooms. Upstairs, there were five larger, more luxurious ones, and at last, he arrived at the last room. He would have purred if tigers could.

Holy shit, the room took up the entire space; there was a claw-foot tub on one end of the room, and just... space. His tiger dropped to the floor and rolled, stretching his paws in the air. Yeah, that would do just fine.

The bed on the other side of the room could have fit his entire pride; his tiger sniffed at it, disinterested. He wouldn't care about it until Aisling was tucked under the covers.

Rye shook his head, wondering if there was something seriously wrong with him. He hadn't decided anything regarding her, damn it. His stupid tiger was pushing his emotions, and needs, to the surface, and making Rye think the Aisling issue was settled, when it really, really wasn't.

Shifting back, he went to the windows, and smiled when he saw that they slid open. There was a tree at eye level; it wasn't exactly near, but he thought he could make the leap. He'd find out soon.

Some might have found it suicidal, but being a shifter thankfully came with an accelerated healing rate; if he broke his leg, it would take a day to heal, at most. As they had Ola, it could be sorted in less than an hour.

RYE TURNED, hearing steps approaching; Tracy stood at his door, holding his phone up.

"There's a missed call. Unknown number. I figured, with everything going on, you might want to know sooner rather than later."

He hurried to her, but the young enforcer hid it behind her back, smirking.

"Just look at you, Rye! I didn't even know you *could* smile."

Dammit; she was right - there he was, smiling. Again.

"You think it's her, don't you?"

He played dumb, lifting one eyebrow, which only served to make Tracy roll he eyes.

"Aisling. Badass, mysterious, sexy loner extraordinaire."

"Give me my phone, Tracy."

He used to be good at sounding pissed off.

"Nope. Not yet. I have to say something, because boys are dumb and you probably won't work it out until next decade or so. You've changed - a lot. We're in a completely fucked up situation, but you're happy when she's around, Rye. I don't think we've ever seen you this…positive. So, some of us - not naming and shaming, but *some of us* - think that she may very well be your mate."

"It's crossed my mind. But it may just be that she has a fucking amazing ass."

"Maybe. I don't know, let's try something okay?"

"Not okay," he growled, but Tracy had a tendency to take orders as suggestions, unless he pulled rank; which he practically never did.

"Just tell me out loud. Say, *Aisling isn't my mate*. That shouldn't be hard, right?"

Rygan opened his mouth to say just that, in order to get the annoying girl off his back, but his tiger roared before a word had passed his lip, refusing to let him lie.

Mine. Ours.

Holy fucking shit.

He blinked, taken aback, utterly confused.

"That's what I thought."

Tracy was still smirking, indifferent to the fact that his world had just turned off its axis, collapsed, and been rebuilt in a split second. He could still try to deny it, but it wasn't going to convince anyone, least of all him.

Aisling - Aisling No Fucking Name - was his fated mate.

"Give me my phone, Tracy."

His tone was pleading now. She heard it, and finally relinquished the device.

Rye dialed back the number which had just called his, feeling like someone had punched his gut, when her voice answered after the fourth ring.

"Hey."

That was it, just *hey*. But it was his mate he was talking to.

Her voice sounded different over the phone, softer maybe. Might just have been because she wasn't glaring with that expression that made him think she was considering whether she wanted to talk to him, or kick him in the nuts.

"Hey back."

His voice somehow didn't break.

Rye wasn't good at the small talk thing, so he jumped right into it without prelude. "We have news about the Vergas pack. You won't like it."

He didn't think he could find anything about the situation even remotely entertaining, but he'd been wrong. When she was pissed, Ace was pretty inventive with her use of profanity. *Fucking shitty cocksucking hell* was his personal favorite.

Sassy. Passionate. Protective. Crazy. *His*.

"They need to go down," she said in a growl.

"Agreed. I'll contact my father, my brother and basically everyone I can think of. My family and I aren't on the best terms, so I don't know how that will go, though."

"I've already made a few calls," Ace told him, making him smile. She really was in this with the rest of them.

Of course she was.

Rye might have let her leave it at that, before his world had changed, but not now. Now, he wanted in. He needed her to lower her defenses, and open up to him.

"Ace, I know you're used to doing your own thing, plan stuff out yourself - but I need to know what you have on this. Talk to me, sweetheart."

She was silent on the other end of the phone for a while; but then, she talked.

"I don't have much to say right now. I got in touch with a dozen friends; they'll come down whenever they can. They're all loners, for the record. But I trust them, and they are dangerous motherfuckers." She marked a pause for a few seconds. "None of them are felines. Will that be a problem?"

"No," he was adamant. "We'd appreciate help from anyone."

They weren't exactly at liberty to be picky. Besides, the ideologies of the backward pack tracking them made a fact hit home: it didn't matter what breed they were, what status they had. Hybrids, submissives, dominants. Who cared? They were all individuals. He loved the shit out of their little Lola Bear, and she apparently was half wolf.

The silence stretched out again; not exactly uncomfortable, but it was probably time to say goodbye and hang up. Finding it impossible to do so, he asked, "How was your day?"

If he sounded awkward, that was because he had no fucking clue what he was doing; small talk started like that, right?

"Uneventful. Having the house to myself feels weird - but the animals came back, though, so I'm not alone."

"You're welcome here anytime, Ace. You don't have to feel lonely."

"There's a difference between lonely and alone, Rye."

"Nevertheless, we'd love to have you around."

She was uncomfortable, he could tell - that was good news. If she hadn't wanted to be anywhere near them, he was pretty sure she would just have said so. The woman wasn't known for mincing her words.

"So, tell me," he said, still reluctant to hang up, "What makes Aisling tick?"

"Why do you ask? You don't need to know in order to get into my pants, if that's what it's about."

Yeah…no one said it was supposed to be easy. Short

of blurting out, *you're my mate, damn it!* he didn't know what to say.

He couldn't say it, not now. There was a good chance that the stubborn woman would laugh in his face; he needed to give her time to sense it herself. Nothing in the way she behaved made him think she might suspect that they were true mates.

"I want to fuck you - as you're well aware. But I'd also like to get to know you."

She took a few second to think.

"I like books."

"What genres?"

He expected her to be into gore, horror, or maybe sci-fi.

"Romance; steamy, funny or cheesy- I'm not fussy. Shifter romance always makes me laugh."

"What else."

"I don't think so mister. We said you get one question, I get one, remember?"

Oh, yes. He recalled that evening; in graphic detail.

"So we did. Ask away."

She did. She wanted to know his favorite color, he then asked what she liked to eat. He wasn't sure how long they stayed on the phone, when Ian came to let him know that Jas had made it home.

"I've got to go, Ace. Call you tomorrow."

Rygan took a second to breathe after hanging up. He'd just spend an hour getting to know his mate.

His fucking *mate*.

"What's the matter with you?"

So, Tracy hadn't told on him yet.

Good. It gave him some time to get his shit together.

CLUB

*S*he never understood why so many shifters loved clubs. The music was too loud, the air too clouded with perfume, sweat and pheromones. She bore it when she wanted to find someone to fuck, but that couldn't be any further from her mind today. Her cat hissed at males trying to rub themselves against her, refusing to even look at them, because they weren't Rygan Wayland.

But the girls had asked, and then, pouted when she'd said no. What had convinced her was the fact that the world was a dangerous place, when Vivicia Crawley, Faith Howell, and Rain Philips were bored and horny.

So there she was, in the middle of the dancefloor, dancing with the wolf, the raven, and the witch who'd been the first to answer her call. They lived down in California, just a few hours away, so Ace had expected them to arrive before everyone else. She just hadn't thought that they'd drop everything they were working on and rush to her aid immediately.

Although she should have expected just that. Ace didn't form friendships easily, but when she did, it was with people who were loyal to a fault. She would have jumped into a car, or a plane, if any of them had asked for her help - it wasn't surprising that they'd done it for her.

She'd briefed them on the situation, and they'd expressed their feelings differently, in manners that reflected their personalities. Vivicia had shifted and gone out to hunt something down, Faith went to her laptop and checked out the closest gun shop in the area, while Rain had started smiling because she didn't often have the leisure of using more than a sliver of her powers. This time, she was pretty sure no one would begrudge her for killing everything in her path.

When the exotic beauty with long golden limbs came back, a rabbit in hand, blood all over her naked skin, she announced, "We're going out tonight. We'll meet your pride in the morning."

Vivicia often took charge. She wasn't the most dominant of them, but Faith generally didn't care, and Rain ignored what she didn't want to do. Out of the four of them, Ace was the only who went against Vivicia - normally, the others took her side, but in this instance, they all agreed that they needed to wind down before it all started. So there they were, at the club.

"Try touching my ass again and you won't have a finger left," she growled at the idiot who wasn't taking a hint.

"Come on, sweetheart, chill."

Why didn't they listen? Ace grabbed the idiot by the throat and threw him at the nearest wall. In another club, that might have been noticed, but they were at Trance, the most popular sup club in Portland. There was a fight breaking out every other hour, on a quiet night.

"I'll go get some air," she shouted in Vivicia's ear, before making her way through the sea of bodies, to get to the smoker area behind the club.

She'd never been a club bunny, but she hadn't hated them before either; now, she really, *really* did. Or rather, she hated feeling all those males touching her.

What the fuck? Aisling was no prude. Shifters needed sex and she made no apologies for it. Sure, she wasn't easy, and she never settled for anyone she didn't fancy - but tonight, she hadn't even been looking. Normally, the males she didn't want bored her. They didn't infuriate her like they did today.

She'd known her cat - and herself, if she was sincere - wanted Rye, but she hadn't realized that it wanted no one else.

Maybe she could ask Rain if there was a potion against that.

Ace grabbed the phone ringing in her pocket and rolled her eyes when she saw the name flashing on the screen; Rygan. Of course.

"Good evening."

Being an alpha male, the man immediately asked, "What's that noise in the background? Where are you?"

And as she was Ace Cross, she shot back, "What makes you think you have the right to know?"

"Aisling."

His tone was warning her; she found it amusing.

"Aww. You really do think you can intimidate me. Look at you, still delusional."

"Where are you?" he growled threateningly.

"None of your business. Any reason why you called?"

He did manage to surprise her, by just hanging up on her. She was still staring at the phone in disbelief when it rang again.

"Trance, Aisling? Really?"

She had a positively awesome snarky repartee at the ready, so she sighed when he hung up again.

Aisling spent the next hour considering whether she

should text him, call him back - and maybe tease him for being so easily ruffled - or just wait until morning, when she felt a presence behind her.

She hadn't seen that coming at all, believing that he'd be completely focused on his territory and his pride, yet there was no mistaking that particular musk, or the way her cat behaved when she smelled it.

"Rye."

She didn't have to turn to know it was him.

"What are you doing here, Ace?" he sounded frustrated, yet resigned. Hopefully, he'd come to terms with the fact that he didn't have the authority to boss her around.

"And that's your problem, because?"

She knew she probably shouldn't push his buttons, but it was just so much *fun*.

Rye walked around her and pinned her under his intense gaze again. She managed to prevent herself from squirming, but only just.

"Because I care about you. And because, for now, I consider you mine."

She snorted, which served to amuse him. The Alpha took another step, getting right in her personal space, and leaned towards her.

"You want to play this game? Fine. I'll go in right now,

grab the first girl who throws herself at me and screw her in the restroom. How would you like that?"

She knew he was just playing her, she *knew* it, and she should have been able to shrug indifferently - but before her brain had kicked in, her cat was hissing and digging her claws into his arm, almost deep enough to mark.

"That's what I thought."

"You're an asshole."

"You like it in the asshole? Good to know."

She groaned. "Please, Rygan- I swear I'll tell you whatever you want to know. Just don't ever attempt to joke again."

He smiled, relaxed, and started playing with her hair. Strangely, she let him.

"A few friends of mine made it early. Only three of them, but they're going to make a difference, even if no one else turns up."

"I know. Daunte is here - he recognized one of the girls. He's currently trying to chat her up."

That made Ace wince. Daunte had tried to get into Vivicia's pants for years - she shot him down so harshly each time, Ace was embarrassed on his behalf.

"So what made you crash our girls night out?"

"I might not have, if you'd just told me it was a girls night out."

Touché.

"I didn't think you'd leave your territory, with everything happening right now."

"Jas came back - she, Ian, Coveney, Ola, and Tracy can handle things for an hour. We're not far."

She nodded, then, because she was pretty sure he wouldn't catch the drift without a hint, she added, "You know, I would probably be a little less difficult if you didn't attempt to boss me around."

He shrugged unapologetically. "I'll still try. You'll shoot me down each time. Might as well get used to it. Come on. Dance with me, pretty cat."

SURPRISE

*U*nsurprisingly, she felt right against him, her body fitting perfectly as they moved together; there were a good two hundred people in the club, but they might as well have been alone in the universe.

Rye caressed her arms, her back, her ass, exploring his mate. When he couldn't stop himself from doing so, he tilted her head up, and kissed her plump lips. Not only did she let him- she responded touch for touch, and leaned closer to him, her soft curves pushed against his hard flesh.

"I'm going to take you home tonight." It wasn't a question. "I'll make you scream my name so loud the entire town won't doubt you're mine."

"Get it right, pretty boy," the vixen replied, biting his lip playfully. "*I'm* getting you home, as there are no sensitive ears at my place. And you'd *better* make me scream."

Fuck. She was so fucking perfect for him - the very first woman who'd ever dared to speak up to him.

"Holy fuck, Ace!" that came from a feminine voice close by; Rye was too busy nipping at his mate's neck to care enough to check whose.

"Wanna introduce me to your *friend?*"

The voice sounded flirty and to his amusement, Aisling growled a warning.

"Oh. Right. Well, that explains things. Catch you later!"

Rye smiled against her skin, but didn't say a word. He didn't need to. His little mate was slowly under-standing what Tracy had made him realize; he could wait…as long as she didn't take too long to understand she was his.

"That was Rain, by the way. She's a witch - a good one. We'll get her to place specific wards around your home tomorrow."

Her tone was curt.

"She's a friend of yours, then."

"Yes?"

She didn't sound quite sure about that.

"Yet you growl at her because she sounds interested in me…"

"I will kick you in the balls if you mention that again."

"You're possessive- we both are. Can you imagine how much more we will be once I've pounded this pussy all night long, Aisling?"

"Or, maybe that will be enough to get it out of our system."

He bit her earlobe a little harder than necessary, punishingly. Ace shivered and plastered herself against him.

"You like that, do you?"

Teasing her always had consequences; he wasn't sure what she'd do but he expected retaliation.

Yet, she shocked him by gliding her hand right inside his pants, underneath his boxers, and firmly grabbing his throbbing cock; she pumped it twice, and flickered her finger over the sensitive head, before pushing up on her tiptoes, and getting to his ear.

"You like that, do you?" she parroted in a soft whisper, before nibbling at his ear.

Fucking hell.

Enough nonsense. He just grabbed her, threw her on his shoulder, and called to his Beta, "Daunte, we're going. Now."

Aisling's friends, who he still hadn't been introduced to, left with them. Two of them sat with them at the back of the pride SUV, the other one sat at the front. Ace spent the whole way on top of him, grinding against him, biting and licking, like they were alone in the world. He hadn't taken her for an exhibitionist, but she was proving him wrong.

Good. He wanted the world to see she was *his*.

Daunte offered to drive, saying, "I really don't want to see you guys going at it."

He really did seem disgusted, which was strange, because Daunte was *really* into watching people fuck.

Rye was a little too preoccupied to analyze it, trying not to come in his pants.

"I'm going to plunge inside that hot pussy the moment we're alone," he told Ace, cupping her under her short shorts.

Fuck, she was already so damn wet.

"I don't see why you're waiting," one of the girls said. "You're basically fucking anyway."

They were. Ace had taken his cock out, and never stopped touching it.

"Fabric interior. Cleaning cum is a bitch," he replied with a shrug.

Finally - *finally* - Daunte, who'd been driving way

above the limit the last few miles, swerved in front of the house and they burst out of the car.

They didn't make it indoor. Aisling's hands, partially shifted, teared through his clothes, and he took it as an invitation to do the same. Fucking hell, she was perfect, with her small, firm tits he wanted to suck and bite and lick…

He did just that, bending down to reach them, while pushing his desperate cock deep inside his mate's drenched heat.

Rye stayed still one infinite instant, not quite under-standing everything he felt; his insides were exploding, his heart contracted and the tiger inside him roared, hard. He felt her claws deep inside his back - these *would* mark, and leave scars. They were meant to. So would the marks he'd made on her forearms, without consciously choosing to do so. He'd drawn blood. He'd claimed her; and she'd claimed him right back.

"What. The. Hell."

He should have felt sorry for her; she was only now realizing the force at work. But Rye just laughed, and drew his dick back before plunging harder inside her, making her cry out in pleasure and pain. Then, he did it again, and again, and again, until she was panting, whimpering, chanting *please*.

They came together in under ten minutes- in other circumstances, it would have been embarrassing.

Still panting like he'd finished a sprint, Ace then glared, accusingly saying, "You don't look surprised."

Rye just shrugged, particularly self-satisfied. There was no denying that out of the two of them, she normally had the upper hand. She had more contacts, she was better at subtle shit - he hadn't even guessed that Lola, the kid he'd looked after since she was a newborn, had wolf in her, yet one sniff, and Aisling knew.

But for all this, the woman had been completely blind about the one thing that mattered between them.

"Surprised by what?" he asked playfully, yet seriously.

He needed to hear her say it.

Aisling rolled her eyes, but she must have sensed what he wanted, because she spelled it out. "You're my true mate."

Damn right he was. He ruffled her wavy hair and kissed her forehead. "And you're mine. Now get your pretty ass up."

He got to his feet and lent her a hand to help her up. "There's about eleven rooms I need to fuck you in inside this house. Better get to it."

MARKS

*H*e genuinely didn't think anything could cloud this day for him, so in its infinite wisdom, the world proved him wrong.

Rye woke up feeling that his pridemates were anxious; not terrified or desperate, but still feeling uneasy. He opened his eyes and turned to the soft, perfect body of his mate, next to him under the covers, and kissed her shoulders.

She had a few bruises - so did he. They hadn't gone easy on each other; claimings were messy affairs, but their healing rate meant that they'd be history by the afternoon. What caught his attention were the marks on her arms. Instead of looking like she'd been clawed, intricate patterns had appeared on her skin; they were ocean blue, and changed like running water.

Beautiful.

Rye dreaded to have to tell her that he needed to go, when all he wanted was staying with her and burying himself deep within her folds again, but he didn't have to.

"There's something wrong with your pride, right?"

Of course. Now he paid attention, he felt her through the pride link. He hadn't noticed at first because she hadn't joined as someone he should take care of, look after. She wasn't one of his cats. She was his equal. Their Alpha female. He'd only hear her when she wanted him to.

"Our pride, pretty girl."

Aisling tensed a little.

"They all respect you, Ace. And most of them like you, too. You'll fit in, because you were made for it."

As she didn't answer, he pushed, "You know it, don't you? That you're a born Alpha. No one with your level of dominance would ever be content to live alone."

"My father also is a born Alpha. So is Daunte, for that matter. None of them rule a pride."

"Daunte *is* the highest pack authority after me. And he can obey me, because he knows I'm more dominant than him." To be fair, he admitted, "Slightly, anyway. But you're missing the point. He *is* part of a pride."

Aisling sighed. "Well, nothing we can do about it now. We'll see how it plays out."

She wasn't exactly ecstatic, but she hadn't asked him to leave the pride, so there was that.

He worried all of a sudden, because honestly, if she couldn't deal with living within the Wyvern pride…he would leave with her. He had no other choice on the matter.

Shaking his head, he put that thought out of his mind and got up. They had more pressing worries right now.

"They're coming our way, I can feel them getting closer. Have you got any clothes my size?"

"Yeah, Daunte has some stuff in the guest bedroom, next door. Help yourself."

They got dressed and he headed downstairs just in time: Jas, Coveney, Daunte and Ian arrived on her front porch, in animal form.

All of them stopped dead, and shifted.

"Holy fuck."

"I knew it!"

"Seriously?"

Rye smirked. The mating bond had changed him, he knew it; he felt quieter, more confident. He couldn't quite place it; obviously, though, his pride could tell the difference.

"Dude you were always scary but you basically look like a freak now. Have you *seen* your eyes?"

He hadn't; turning to the closest window, he smiled at his reflection. Freak was right. His normally grey eyes had been replaced by cold, electrifying blue pupils and the marks she'd started on his back had changed, forming patterns that would look like tattoos if they hadn't been blazing amber, like liquid fire was running through his skin.

He rather liked it.

"So, she was your mate. How unexpected," Daunte said. Yet, the man was smirking smugly. "And I believe that means I win our little bet, guys. You all owe me and Tracy two-fifty for the mate thing, and two-fifty because they've fucked within a week. Pay up."

Rye just shook his head; so *that* was why Tracy had given him a nudge. Devious little thing.

While he was happy about the mating, now wasn't the time to linger on it. Ace came down from upstairs, fully dressed; she'd also taken a shower, washing his scent off. He didn't like that bit, but he'd remedy it soon enough.

His three Enforcers and his Beta bowed down as she came to stand next to him, hands over their heart, silently showing their acceptance of her as their Alpha female now. He felt how awkward Aisling was, so he moved on to get to the point.

"I felt something through the pride link?"

The others stopped joking around, instantly growing somber.

"Yes. Kim is gone," Jas said.

The instant the words crossed her lips, Rye realized that the most useless member of his pride wasn't anywhere. And by that, he didn't mean to say she'd popped out in town. He also couldn't *feel* her, not even faintly. As he was the Alpha, he felt every member of his pride.

That could only mean one thing. She'd left the pride.

If that had happened to any other one of his cats, he would have noticed it immediately, but as the useless, passive one he paid no attention to, she'd slipped by unnoticed. He'd had a great many things to think about of late.

"Fuck."

"She left before I came back," Jas added. "We waited all night - I figured she might just be out partying or something - but when I called this morning, she said she wasn't coming back, and hung up on me."

She didn't sound surprised, or upset for that matter. Nevertheless, Rye felt responsible.

"I'm sorry Jas, I have no clue when that happened - she never said anything."

If she had come to him, he might have tried to dissuade her from leaving, for Jas's benefit.

Maybe.

His Enforcer shook her head, "No, *I'm* sorry for asking you to let her in the pride. I keep hoping, but you know some people are just…"

Neither of them completed that sentence. Kim was a shallow, egocentric, megalomaniac pain in the ass, and they were well rid of her, if Jas didn't mind.

"So, you're not going to go after her?"

Jas shrugged. "No. This pride is my home." She didn't elaborate but he saw what she meant: it had never been Kim's.

"I'm sorry we didn't manage to make her feel welcome."

"We did," Ian replied growling. "She just wasn't into the pride thing. She preferred doing what she liked, when she liked. Living in the human world. That's fine. That's how she was raised, and pride life just doesn't suit everyone."

It wasn't the Enforcer's fault, but Rye could have strangled him for saying it in front of Ace; she tensed, feeling that the words could apply to her, too. Another problem for another time.

"Right. Well, as your sister, she'll have our protection if she ever needs it. We have bigger issues - the Vergas wolves. Three of Ace's friends have joined us; did Daunte introduce you?"

Jas smiled. "Yeah, they're fun."

Oh dear. If Jas liked them, they *were* seriously dangerous then.

"Good. We're still outnumbered, though. Any news from our allies?"

"I have to check our messages, but three Alphas answered yesterday. We have their backing. Your brother said he's passed the message on to your dad." Which could mean anything.

"Right. Better get ready, then."

SCOUTS

They had a solid plan and every day more allies pledged their help, so Rygan learned to relax, more or less.

He, Ace, and their Enforcers patrolled around the clock, barely taking the time to sleep. Ace still popped her head in at her bakery, which meant that she was more exhausted than all of them combined, although she did leave quite a few responsibilities up to her assistant.

The nice, always cheerful girl actually became an important part of the pride. The day after their claiming, Rygan was with her when Ace went to dismiss her, regretfully.

"You're an awesome employee, but we're in the middle of a fucking mess, and you can't get involved. I'm not firing you; let's just call it a paid leave."

"No fucking way," the girl had replied.

Ace reasoned with her, making her understand that just working for her, having their scent around her, was putting a target on her back because, for lack of better word, she was weak.

"I'm not letting those fanatics fuck with my life," she replied, stubbornly crossing her arms on her torso. "And if you're going to concentrate on the security around town, you need me here."

She didn't budge, so Rygan ordered that someone would guard the bakery at all times when Ace wasn't in.

Clarissa learned some of Ace's most popular recipes and took over the accounting; they hired a driver to do the rounds she used to do before. She also updated the website and he was infinitely grateful to her for taking some stuff off his mate's shoulders.

The girl also was popular with the rest of his pride because every day before going home, she stopped by their place with all the leftovers.

The only one who didn't seem to have taken to her was, strangely, Daunte. The guy was normally easygoing, but he constantly glared at the poor kid.

"Hey everyone!" she sang out, walking in their lounge, a large tray in hand.

The kids were already halfway down the stairs, running to her.

"We had an awesome day at the shop, so there wasn't much left. I've just made a batch of pies for you guys, though."

Everyone thanked her; Daunte grunted.

"You look nice today," Ola complimented her.

She did; Clary was normally a jeans and t-shirt gal, but today she wore a sundress, and some make up, too.

"I had a lunch date."

"Nice! How did it go?"

They went on talking about girly shit, so Rye turned back to Daunte; he'd just returned from his shift with Ace.

The two often patrolled together, and Rye tried not to be offended by it, but honestly, it hurt. His mate never ran with him in her animal form; he hadn't been sure at first, but it had been three weeks now, and not once had they been rotated in together. He was pretty sure she did it on purpose.

"Nothing to report. Ace just went to grab a few more boxes from her house."

She was taking her time moving - another thing that annoyed him to no end.

Rye nodded, and headed out of doors for his turn, when his phone rang.

"Hey pretty girl."

"The wards have been triggered," was Ace's tense reply.

It wasn't the first time that the wards Rain had set up around town were activated; every time one of their allies stopped by to speak to them, the pride stressed out just as much, thinking that it could be it - their attack.

Rye had enough of waiting for it. If anything, he was actually eager to getting it over with now.

"We're on our way."

He called the fighters currently inside the house. Christine took the kids to the kitchen, and he saw Clary standing nearby, at a loss.

"Someone passed the wards. You know the drill. Everyone out - we need to separate and find out who came as soon as possible."

They'd done it many times, so he didn't think there was anything to discuss, but Daunte said, "Someone should stay back. In case there *is* an enemy, we don't want the house to be undefended."

Rygan frowned. They'd discussed it before and decided that, as the house was pretty hard to get into unnoticed, sending everyone out would be more efficient.

Suddenly, Rye understood what he'd missed. Daunte wasn't exactly *against* the pretty assistant, after all.

"It's a five minute job, Daunte. We'll be back in no time - and quicker if we all go out. Besides, it's probably just another ally."

After a while, Daunte nodded, and they went out.

The last twenty times the very same thing had occurred, they'd found the intruder easily, because they hadn't wanted to sneak in. When five minutes passed without him getting any message from his Enforcer, his mate, or his Beta, Rye shifted and sent a message through the pride link.

Ace, you know what to do. The rest of us, back to the pride house now.

HE WAS RUNNING towards their home when a strong vibe running through the pride link made him stop. This time, the disturbance through the pride link wasn't minor.

Shit.

He was close by now, in the forest right behind the house, close enough to hear some commotion.

Shit.

Ace and Daunte were the first to join him, followed by their Enforcers.

"I can smell wolves," Ace whispered softly.

Rye nodded stiffly.

Fuck, he couldn't believe he'd been stupid enough to take his best men with him, leaving the pride defenseless just like it always was in Hsu's vision.

"How did they get in without notice? As well as the wards, there's the security codes, and everything."

He'd like to know that too, but it wasn't his biggest concern.

"They're making a racket. Chances are, they haven't found Lola yet," Daunte guessed. "Hsu might be hiding her."

Probably; the little girl was smart, and with Niamh's help, she might have managed to cloak their hide out. Still, she was only buying them time. They needed to get in.

Daunte turned to Ace, speaking directly to her. "There are a dozen wolves in there. If we barge in, they'll slaughter our kids, your assistant, and Christine."

They stared at each other, glaring defiantly, and all of a sudden, Ace removed her jacket and threw it at his face.

"Fuck you, Daunte. Fuck you *very much.*"

The guy smirked as she removed layer after layer of clothing; if he didn't know better, Rye would have thought he was gay, because he didn't even look at her fucking perfect ass and her sweet, firm tits once, content to carry on smiling like a doofus.

Then, a familiar bone breaking sound resounded, as the female shifted.

To their credit, none of them laughed, although it might have been because they were in shock.

The intimidating as fuck, strong, dominant, and all around badass woman they all knew and feared changed into his sweet little kitty cat - the one he'd ran with, the one who let him pet her and purred to his touch. She was bigger than a domestic cat, but not by much.

They only had the time to gawk for a split second when the adorable little kitty climbed the closest tree and ran along its branches, jumping to the next, and then the next, until she'd reached the tree situated right in front of his bedroom. The jump was long - he hadn't been sure he'd manage it himself, but she cleared it seemingly effortlessly.

Fierce and cute as fuck. That was his girl.

"I can't believe she shifted in front of *all of you* so quickly."

Daunte sounded elated, and shocked. He could understand why; she had probably come across way too many assholes who'd made fun of her over the years. That explained why she was so set against prides.

Rye turned to Ian, Coveney, Jas, Ola and Tracy.

"If any of you make her feel bad…"

"Not happening," was Ian's response, coming as a growl. "She's protecting our cubs right now. We'll tease her, because that's what pridemates do. But none of us are going to bully our Alpha female."

Nods all around. Although most of them were trying pretty hard to keep their amusement under control.

The noises in the house changed; instead of tearing the place upside down, the intruders had started fighting, which was their cue to getting inside.

Rye shifted, along with the rest of his pride, and they ran towards their home.

Getting in took three minutes and by the time they'd made it, ten wolves were crawling on the floor, incapacitated, maimed, or with broken legs and arms, another one was dead, while the last was struggling under Ace's heel. She'd shifted back; naked, and covered in blood, the woman looked like a warrior goddess from ancient times. His dick twitched, finding the whole thing sexy as fuck, which was probably a little disturbing.

He glanced around and found every member of his pack, barring Hsu, Niamh and Lola. He didn't worry, feeling them through the pride link; they were okay.

She didn't take the time to finish them off because she wanted to get all of them, Daunte sent through the pride link. *We need to do the clean-up.*

They went to the wolves, snapping necks and biting arteries out, before shifting back to their original form.

Nakedness was pretty standard for most shifters, but Rye immediately went to grab his jacket and dropped it on Ace's shoulder, his tiger and he in agreement: they didn't want anyone else to look at what was *his*.

"Efficient as usual, sister," Daunte said.

He went right to Clarissa, and wordlessly pushed her hair out of the way, then moved her arms, and turned her around, checking everything was still in place. Once he was satisfied she was alright - if a little in shock - he turned his back on her and went to the kitchen.

Meanwhile, Rye and the others were feeling like idiots.

Sister.

There was no doubt that he'd meant that literally; Ace *was* his sister.

"I can't believe I didn't see it. You're it. Him. The Butcher's first child."

"Dude, how dumb are we? They act like siblings. They even smell similar, fuck it."

Ace shrugged while they picked their jaws up.

"The kids are hiding somewhere. Any idea where?"

Christine was shaken, but she pointed towards the game room tucked under the staircase.

Rye didn't see anything when he got in, but he knew they were there. Seconds later, they appeared right in front of their eyes.

He smiled at Niamh, and took Lola off her hands.

"Good job, little witch. Well done protecting your sisters."

The poor girl looked like she might faint, but she'd done as well as any adult Enforcer might have in her place. Some day - soon - he could imagine her joining the pride authority.

"Here come my best girls," Daunte chirped when they walked in the lounge, a tray of hot chocolate and cookies in his arms.

The Beta distributed the goodies to all the kids first, then Clarissa, before offering the rest to the Enforcers.

Once the shock had passed, the fighters assembled, and Rye asked Ace, "Is everything ready?"

His mate nodded.

They knew it was coming any minute now. These wolves had just been scouts, and they'd indubitably contacted their packs.

By morning, they would have war.

FAMILY

They took the kids with them, and waited in a clearing by the lake. Anyone passing by might have thought it was just a group of young people having a nice picnic by the water with their children. They weren't wrong, really. Ian had made some sandwiches, Clarissa had baked some stuff and tagged along, because Daunte had - privately, when she was out of hearing range - insisted that she was too close to them to be left behind. All in all, they were actually having a lot of fun.

Ace knew her brother; he liked the girl - a lot. Watching that unfold was going to be a lot of fun. Daunte wasn't normally serious with women, so, he was going to mess up. Epically.

Now that Ace had shifted, she felt more comfortable doing so again. No one had said a bad word about her being what she was: an animal. No one seemed disgusted either. She hadn't realized just how frightened she was of never being accepted because of her nature, until they'd made it a non-issue.

Although now, Daunte called her sis ever other second, making up for all the times when she hadn't let him.

To get even, Ace secretly smirked, glancing at her brother before asking Clary, "How was your date yesterday, by the way?"

If she wasn't mistaken, there was a low growl coming from her left. Hilarious.

"Ugh, the worst. The guy wouldn't stop talking about how important his work is. He's a damn *bank clerk*, for Christ's sake!"

She was laughing when suddenly, the atmosphere around them changed. Aisling got up, alongside the rest of her pride.

Holy shitty fuckity hell.

They approached as one, appearing at the other end of the clearing all of a sudden; they obviously had a witch cloaking them. A good one.

She knew that there were hundreds of Vergas wolves, but she hadn't expected them all to come, leaving their territory undefended. But they had, which was telling her how serious they were about their insane cause.

Ace immediately spotted the Alpha. A middle-age, handsome man with salt and pepper hair, walking like the world belonged to him. He was completely naked, and hard, too- he liked this. The idea of destroying a small pride with children excited him.

She recognized the woman standing at his left. Ace didn't feel one way or another about it, but from the unanimous growl coming from her pridemates, she was the only one who didn't take offense.

Kim- Jas' twin. She'd betrayed them. That explained how the scouts had made it past their security. They hadn't changed the security codes, and they'd even got Rain to allow her to pass through her wards like the rest of the pride, using some hair they'd found on her pillow to make sure she could come back if she so wanted. With her blessing, the wards wouldn't have had any effect on the wolves.

"I can't believe it."

"I can," Jas spit. "From what she told me over the phone when I talked to her last, she was pretty pissed when Rygan refused to fuck her. I thought she was going to get over it...but she's just not that mature."

Now, Ace was growling too, and also baring her teeth. The plastic Barbie had wanted *her mate?* That was another matter altogether.

"You realize we're going to kill her for this, right?" Daunte asked.

Jas laughed. "Get in line."

The humongous pack stopped fifteen feet away, at their Alpha's wave. The man then advanced, flanked by two younger men, both of whom looked like him.

Power stayed in the family, then.

They walked right to Ace and Rye, appraising their marks.

"A mated pair."

The Alpha wolf seemed approving. Of course he would be: being dominant and mated made them strong, and that was the thing that mattered most to him. Ace wondered what he'd say if he saw her shifting.

"I'm Arthur. These are my Beta and Head Enforcer, as well as my sons, Jason and Hunter."

Ace wanted to roll her eyes. *Hard.* Really? They were exchanging civilities? She had to give him that, though: the man did hide his psychopath tendencies pretty well.

One of his sons, however? Not so much. The idiot Arthur had called Hunter winked at her. Ace had to physically restrain Rye.

Arthur had the decency to scowl at his Head Enforcer.

"Look, there's no need to fight here. All we want…"

"We know what you want," Rye replied as conversationally. "It's not going to happen. Lola is one of us."

"Lola, is it?" the Alpha laughed. "You see, I actually understand you. She just looks like a little kid now, but in ten years, when she shifts... do you know what she'll look like, then?"

Rye shrugged.

"An animal. Like the rest of us."

"A monster," Arthur amended. "Twice the size of any wolf, quicker, more agile than any feline, and at war with herself. She'll go feral, like so many of her kind have before- and she'll kill. She'll kill your children, your neighbor, you."

Ace and Rye exchanged a glance. They didn't know much about hybrids, but the rumors *did* say that they had a hard time adapting; harder than most shifters, which was saying a lot.

"We'll worry about it when it comes to it."

Arthur looked like he might pity them.

"It'll never come to it. You don't want to condemn your whole pride just for one kid that's not even yours. You're outnumbered - ridiculously so."

Ace smirked, and tilted her head.

"Are we?"

~

THEY'D EXPECTED that the wolves would spy first; giving them enough time to report what they'd found before killing them had always been part of the plan - although they would have preferred if they hadn't stepped a foot inside their home.

The Vergas wolves had come assuming that they'd have the upper hand. Now, she watched their expression morph from casual amusement to gravity as Rain uncloaked herself, and the rest of their allies.

Ace's friends had all made it, with friends of their friends, too. There were two hundred loners of various species, a couple of vampires, as well as Rye's allies - another two hundred strong.

Now they'd been revealed, Byron Wayland walked forward, his older son Colter next to him. They stood on Rye's left side, just as her father, The Butcher, and her stepmother went to stand at her left.

"Rain, take the kids somewhere safe, would you?"

The witch snapped her fingers and smirked as their submissives, Clary, and the kids vanished.

Now Arthur's pleasant demeanor had completely disappeared.

"I get that you're not used to being told no," Rye said. "But you'll never get one of your fucking greasy fingers on Lola, or any other one of our kids. Ever. Now it's up to you. You can turn back, and stay out of our way, or we can end this here and now."

She was pretty certain the man would actually choose the second option, before Rye added, "You might want to know, though, we also have a hundred people ready to burn the fuck out of your territory. That's what you'd planned to do with ours, isn't it?"

The Alpha blanched, making him smile.

"You're welcome to burn our empty, fully insured house. We'll settle down elsewhere. But moving five hundred and twenty seven adults, as well as three hundred and four kids from the home they've inhabited for seven generations might be a little bit more of an issue, I'm sure."

Coveney had come through with plenty of intel.

The Vergas Alpha walked forward, but his sons grabbed his arms, and leaned in to whisper, evidently attempting to reason with him.

Finally, he turned to them, rage evident in his eyes.

"This isn't over."

"Isn't it?" Byron asked, his beaming voice full of humor. "Because I'm telling you right now: you attack my son again? I'll take it as a personal offense against our crown. I'll come down on you with everything I've got."

Yeah… he might seem a little gruff and all, but Ace didn't mind her mate's father.

But if she loved the dad, she completely adored the grandmother.

"Excuse me?" a sweet little frail voice interjected, as the Alpha wolf began to retreat.

They all turned to the petite old lady with long silver hair, who was pointing past the Alpha, towards Kim.

"That filthy piece of shit. We want it. Consider it our due for letting you go without declaring war on your ass, will you?"

The wolf growled, but he nodded towards Hunter, who went to grab the traitor, and pushed her their way.

"Why, thank you so much, you pack of savages." Then, she smiled up to Ace and said, "I have a brilliant idea. We can chain her to a tree and get everyone to piss on her before letting her twin rip her throat out."

See? The lady was brilliant. But as entertaining as the visual might have been, Ace had a better idea in mind.

"Actually, I think we should let her go."

Everyone turned to her, staring like she might have lost her mind.

She just smirked, recalling how hard it had been to make it out there on her own.

"We will, of course, notify the human authorities, and

the shifter Council that she's been accused of treason in her pride."

In other words, she would been seen as a piece of trash by shifters, and as a convict by human authorities. The woman was majorly screwed for the rest of her days, just like she deserved to be.

A quick death would have been too kind.

*R*ye didn't think anything could smooth down the issues he had with his family. They'd been too quick to dismiss him during his childhood, and too quick to turn their back on one of their own later in life.

He hadn't realized that when Coveney was proven innocent, they'd all felt like shit. They'd spent the last six years trying to find a way to reach out to him, without success. His asking for help had come as a surprise, and they'd jumped on the chance.

"I always saw how strong you were," Byron told his son. "Colter is steadier, more predictable, and less passionate. As such, he'll make a better leader when I pass on the reins of our kingdom."

Rye nodded; he'd never aspired to be the heir. It seemed like far too much responsibility anyway.

"You, however, are more like your mother. If you see an injustice, you'll jump at the defense of anyone who needs your help without thinking – like you did for your friend Coveney. I should have made it clear that I respected you for it."

His grandmother Maria raised her hand.

"I made it clear! I gave him a hundred grand." Then, she had to add, "For the record, I prefer Colter because he brings me chocolate."

The Wayland family reunion was almost as unbelievable as the Cross one.

"Tell me, is that really the Butcher with a bunch of your kids on his back?"

On all fours, the man was wrestling Clive, Jasper, Victoria, Daniel and Will – and losing, too – while his wife MaryBeth baked stuff that put Ace's desserts to shame in their kitchen.

They looked normal.

"Yep, apparently. Just don't get the catnip out."

Byron had his business face on.

"I wondered if he'd be open to a formal alliance. I know he's no Alpha but having him in our ranks…"

"Your son mated his daughter. You can definitely ask."

HAVING over four hundred people in their territory

was actually not as much of a problem as it might have been elsewhere; they'd just cleaned up the log cabins Aisling never used, and it had accommodated everyone with ease, but after three weeks of having company, Rye was looking forward to spending time with his pride, and his mate.

They knew each other well now; they spend every night in each other's arms, fucking, talking, laughing, and fucking some more. But they'd never had alone time outside of the bedroom. They hadn't gone on a date.

Plus, while they were mated, they hadn't made it official by holding a blood exchange ceremony; every woman out there dreamt of walking down the aisle wearing a pretty dress. And if he was honest with himself, Rye also wanted to officially seal their hands.

"You'll invite us for your ceremony, I hope," his mother said, touching his forearm.

He wasn't surprised that she'd known what he was thinking about; Tara Wayland was an empath, as well as a submissive. She'd stayed behind in case a fight actually broke out.

"Sure."

"I don't think I can say how happy I am that you've actually found your *mate*," she beamed at him. "The feelings around you...I've never experienced this. And your child is going to be so fucking cute. Look at how tiny and adorable Aisling is."

He made a double take, and not only because his mother had said *fucking*.

"Child?"

Did he sound faint? Because he was. He really, really was.

"Oh my…I mean, I don't want to assume but she *feels* like two people. So I just guessed."

Child. They might have a child on the way, an actual piece of him and her.

Yeah. Things were good.

THE END.

HIERARCHY

Wyvern Pride

Rygan – Alpha
Aisling – Alpha
Daunte - Beta
Coveney - Head Enforcer
Ian - Enforcer
Jas - Enforcer
Tracy - Enforcer in training
Ola - Healther
Hsu - Seer
Christine - Submissive
Niamh - Child
Lola - Child
Jasper - Child
Clive - Child
Victoria - Child
Daniel - Child

Will - Child

Royal Pride

Byron – Alpha King
Tara - Alpha Queen
Colter – Head Enforcer

Vergas Pride

Arthur – Alpha
Jason – Beta
Hunter – Head Enforcer

Known Loners

Knox
Vivicia – Wolf
Rain – Witch
Faith – Raven

I hope you enjoyed Kitty Cat.

Next in the series, there will be Daunte's story, Pretty Kitten. Also except a spin off, Hunky Beast, happening between book one and two.

Stay in tune for an excerpt of To Claim a King, my fantasy romance.

TO CLAIM A KING

She'd felt unsteady since dawn, feeling deep in her bones that if she didn't get out of town in time today, she would live to regret it. The young woman, hiding under a well-worn woolen cloak that had been green once, peeked left, then right, checking that no guard was standing near, then stepped out of the shadows and scaled the ten-foot stone wall that surrounded Malec, the small, backward, oppressing town of her birth.

It was the same every day; Xandrie finished her chores, then snuck out the back door, letting the heavy latch down carefully, so no one would be alerted to her departure. Not that any of them cared, to be entirely honest. Her youngest sister knew better than to worry on her behalf, and the others quite simply didn't give a damn. She was the undisputed runt in a family of mages.

Her life might have been easier if she'd come from a clan of ordinary, run-of-the-mill mages, but she hadn't. The members of her family were the most powerful mages for hundreds of miles, according to the talk. People of high birth and bulging wallets came from every corner of the land, to seek a healing poultice or herb-infused draught. They were the best - and twice as ashamed of her for it.

Xandrie scampered up the wall, hand over hand, her feet finding the crevices in the stone from memory. A crow, feathers so black they shone blue, greeted her at the top of the wall. She smiled, waving in its direction before jumping down. She hoisted her bow and quiver over her shoulder, and launched herself off the wall into the soft grass below. Landing in a perfect crouch, she righted herself and stretched her sore limbs, before dashing out towards the tree line, pushing her muscles as far as she could.

She needed it. She had spent her entire day scrubbing floors and polishing silver in preparation for tonight's feast, and her muscles protested against any exertion, but her mind needed the change of pace. When she ran, she forgot everything, even her most pressing worries. Besides, if she was fast enough, she may get to see *them* again.

They'd arrived two days back and taken refuge in an old shelter built of that strange concrete that firmly placed it as a remnant from the previous era; as soon as she'd seen them, she'd known without a shadow of a doubt that she was standing in front of elves.

They were tall, and stood too still to be men, their eyes steady and wise. One of them wore white and blue, the other, red and gold; she found the whole thing tremendously exciting as she knew that the first wore the colors of the house of Aryn, and his companion was dressed like an Elf of Endar - and she knew the two houses were currently at war.

Xandrie sighed in delight, wondering if anything half as exciting had ever happened in this part of the world. She wished she could go right to them and ask their tales, but there was a good chance that one of them would shoot an arrow between her eyes without asking any questions, if they didn't wish to be seen. So, she stayed at a distance, her head full of conjectures.

She'd just arrived at the house, and at first glance, it seemed empty. A shame. Xandrie sighed and tiptoed away, silently turning her heels.

Not silently enough, it would seem.

"Dragon's scale," she cursed, finding a long, curved dagger pointing right at her chin.

"So, here is our little spy."

The voice - and the weapon - belonged to the most beautiful man she'd ever seen. That wasn't saying much, as she'd never left the Var. Their men were known for the love of ale, not their grace and refinement.

The man - or rather, the Elf - had short, dark hair, which wasn't typical of their race. One of his pointed ears was adorned by a sapphire, the same exact blue as his eyes.

He smiled, which shouldn't be allowed because her usually steady knees gave out, and put the sword back in its sheath.

"Don't be too hasty," another voice pitched in, coming from above her head.

Xandrie looked up and a short laugh escaped her lips.

Never mind the first Elf; the platinum blond, long haired one perched on a large branch above ought to have been painted by the finest master.

"She may still be an enemy."

"It's just a girl, Argon."

"A girl with a mouth, and you've just given her my name."

Her eyes popped out of her skull, because she may not be the worldliest woman, but affairs happening beyond her borders fascinated her; whenever strangers passed by her little village, she'd listened, and asked, too. She knew of Argon, the Endar prince who'd been missing for years, and presumed dead.

Holy smoking dragonfire, they were going to slit her throat.

"Are you an agent of the Shadows, and do you intend to sell us out?"

She shook her head vehemently, and replied, "No," for good measure.

"See? She's fine."

The blond-haired prince rolled his eyes. In all honesty, she might have done the same, because his argument was rather flawed - she could have, like, *lied*. But right now, she was all for taking the foolish Elf's side.

"I'm a Truth Seeker, little girl," he told her. "No one can lie to me."

Oh. Well, that changed things. Although, she didn't think there was any Truth Seeker alive, not since…

"And the penny drops."

The last Truth Seeker had been Turin of Aryn, and the man was very much supposed to be dead. He had been killed before her time, and that was the whole reason behind the war that had plagued their kingdoms.

"I'm not going to say a word," she swore, "But, I'm *just a little bit* curious as to why you aren't dead. Both of you."

Xandrie didn't expect either of them to reply; to her

surprise, Turin sat down on the grass next to her, and told her a story about death, evil, and shadows. She sat next to him, listening eagerly. She only understood one word out of two, but she soaked in his voice and imagined the world as they saw it.

"Sixty years ago, I was young and foolish."

"You're still foolish," the second prince interjected.

"I believed my gift meant that I could *always* see the truth. So, when a female Elf…"

"A very sexy female Elf."

"Stop interrupting, or tell the story yourself, dammit!"

Argon shut it.

"When the Elf came to me, saying she needed help - that her realm was in danger - I believed it. I didn't know that my powers don't work on shadows."

"What are shadows?"

The Elf was patient enough to explain it.

"There are four known elements in the world - Earth, Water, Fire, Air - and there is a fifth acknowledged by anyone with a bit of sense."

"Aether," she completed, surprising the Elf. Normal people didn't go around talking about Aether. Before they'd known she had no magics, though, her parents had instructed her well; after, she'd educated herself by sneaking books out of their library when she could.

"Very good. Aether, most know about. But there's also Shadow."

She frowned.

"Think of it as a conscious negative energy. The four basic elements are neutral, and Aether is positive. Shadow thrives when the world is in despair - war, violence feeds it. And just like there are some individuals infused with Aether, Shadow penetrates certain people."

That was rather creepy.

"So, you're saying that this Elf was an agent of evil?"

"Precisely. Anyway, I walked into a trap and I've lived in the Shadow Realm since."

Xandrie's expression said it all: she had no clue what he was talking about.

"He means he's half dead." That made even less sense.

"Our ever cheerful friend here happens to be a child of Aether. He can navigate the Shadow world. He brought me back; as long as I'm with him, I can walk on Eartia."

"So, you're on some sort of a quest to stop the Shadows, right?"

Turin nodded.

Fascinating. Xandrie picked her jaw up, and said the first thing that came to mind.

"How can I help?"

Both Elves looked amused, which could have offended her, if she didn't know just how useless she was - her parents had said that much to her face. Repetitively.

"I don't think I can make a huge difference, but my sister is a powerful mage- I can ask her to create potions for you. I can also buy some supplies; food, maybe?"

The Elves exchanged a glance.

"What's your name, little girl?"

"Alexandria." The grand name wasn't quite her though, so she amended, "Xandrie, really. I go by Xandrie."

"Alexandria, you're generous and stronger than one may think at first. You'll go with our thanks- but we cannot delay our journey further."

Oh. She didn't think they'd stay very long in a forest, next to a village situated right at the opposite of the most exciting point in the world, so she hid her disappointment.

"We'll meet again."

～

Argon watched the child go with a frown. Two days, they stayed in these parts, just in order to observe her.

She could have been an Elf - the way she moved in the wilderness, with grace and respect, wasn't typical of her race.

"We've taken a huge risk with this child," he told his companion.

Turin smirked, shaking his head.

"This is no child, and we did what had to be done. We may have need of her in the future."

He sighed, conceding the point.

"She'll be of little use to us in the Northern Var, so far from where she belongs."

Another truth.

"Come on, Argon. You know what you need to do."

He did. Closing his eyes, he calmed down and felt the world around him, letting the Aether infuse his body and soul.

There she was. Red and magnificent. Eight hundred miles south. The dragon he sought was a day away. He whispered words in a long forgotten tongue until she changed the course of her journey, heading to toward them instead.

"It is done."

Little Alexandria, the first Dragon Rider he'd encountered in his life, would soon meet her fate.

The cries that ricocheted off the castle walls weren't the normal blood-curdling, curse-laden sounds of a woman bringing a new dragonling into the world. No, those birthing howls were generally followed by a blissful hush, some manly back-slapping, and the Order of the Guard's clarion cry from the rooftops, alerting the entire Kingdom of a new arrival.

The screams that had brought the King from his private chambers, were those of a grieving father. Rhey Vasili ruled a Kingdom of great wealth and beauty, which, at its heart, had a profound tragedy: mothers were dying in childbirth.

Rhey powered his way through the Hospital. He pushed past the nurses, batted away the doctors, and threw open the delivery room doors.

The scene could not have been more devastating. A man – the one raising the roof with his guttural groans – had thrown himself across the woman lying on the gurney. The way he clutched at her, begging her to return, said he was the husband and father. The woman lay curled and still, her arm hanging to one side, the sheets around her drenched in blood.

A great beauty with amber skin and emerald eyes stood at the foot of the bed, the newborn dragonling in her arms. Her eyes told Rhey she was beyond sad, beyond pissed, and beyond fed up with the entire situation. "Again, Rhey." Her voice was devoid of any emotion. She'd shut herself off to be able to bear the pain. "It has happened again. She was a good woman, decent and kind; excited to bring a new life into the world and now…now she's…nothing."

Rhey gently took the dragonling from his friend's arms. The tiny creature squirmed and blinked, oblivious to the fact that his mother lay dead not ten feet away. Rhey kissed his forehead, and handed him to a nurse. He put his arm around Princess Demelza, but she wasn't in a state to accept any form of comfort. She wouldn't be for days, or months.

If he had the heart, he would order her to stop attending to these births, but he couldn't. As a noble blood female, blessing the newborns of those sworn to her house was her duty, and her privilege. Kings had no business in these matters. He also knew that while Demelza was barely holding her rage, her calm, regal presence was making everyone else - nurses, doctors, mages, and guards - keep it together.

Rhey did the one thing he could do to ease her burden.

"Go, fly. I'll stay in your stead. The grief won't leave you, but the air under your wings will at least cool your humors."

Demelza briefly kissed his hand, and left the delivery room without a backward glance.

She was right to be enraged. One in two women died in childbirth, leaving scores of orphans and devastated husbands. It hadn't always been that way, according to the tales. Rhey had only walked Earthia for two centuries, but it was said that in the old days, women brought their dragonlings to term without incident. Something had changed, though no one knew what that might be.

"If the damned Elders prioritized this problem, instead of spending their time meddling in my affairs, we might find a solution to this catastrophe."

If the nurses were listening, they didn't let on. Everyone knew the King wasn't happy that the Elders had declared The Claiming would be held at the next full moon, but there was nothing they could do to change how the King's mate was to be chosen, so they went about their work, pretending they hadn't heard a thing.

He felt some shame at lamenting his fate; now wasn't the time, and certainly not the place. Turning to the newly widowed man who didn't even seem to see him, he said, "You'll be excused from your duties indefinitely, and paid your current worth."

The man was now solely responsible for the tiny dragonling getting washed and blessed, and it wouldn't do to let him worry about feeding it.

Eventually, the mages recited the spells, the nurses washed the body and ushered everyone out of the room. Rhey then left the hospital, his ill-humor trailing behind him like plumes of thunder-clouds. He took refuge, as he always did when trouble darkened his doors, atop the endless mountains of shimmering gold that lay beneath the castle.

To Claim a King is available now.

32695671R00121

Made in the USA
Columbia, SC
07 November 2018